THROUGH
THE
WARDROBE

Your Favorite Authors on
C. S. Lewis's Chronicles of Narnia

Edited by Herbie Brennan
with Leah Wilson

AN IMPRINT OF BENBELLA BOOKS, INC.
Dallas, Texas

First BenBella Books edition 2010

Smart Pop is an Imprint of BenBella Books, Inc.
10300 N. Central Expressway, Suite 400
Dallas, TX 75231
www.benbellabooks.com
www.smartpopbooks.com
Send feedback to feedback@benbellabooks.com

Printed in the United States of America
10 9 8 7 6 5 4 3 2 1

Library of Congress Cataloging-in-Publication data is available for this title.
ISBN 978-1935251-68-2

Proofreading by Erica Lovett, Stacia Seaman, and Greg Teague
Cover design by Kit Sweeney
Text design and composition by PerfecType, Nashville, TN
Printed by Bang Printing

Significant discounts for bulk sales are available. Please contact Glenn Yeffeth at glenn@benbellabooks.com or (214) 750-3628.

Contents

Introduction

Something wonderful happens when a group of experienced fiction writers come together to pay tribute to a master. But before we go into that, let me take a moment to introduce those writers to you, in the order they appear in this anthology:

Deb Caletti from San Francisco Bay, now living in the Seattle area . . . **Brent Hartinger**, who hails from just south of Seattle . . . **Diana Peterfreund**, born in Pennsylvania, but lived mostly in Florida . . . **Ned Vizzini**, a Manhattanite who grew up in Brooklyn . . . **Sarah Beth Durst** from central Massachusetts . . . **Herbie Brennan** (that's me), born in Northern Ireland during World War II . . . **Diane Duane**, a New Yorker, now living in Ireland . . . **Kelly McClymer**, who started out in South Carolina and now lives in Maine . . . **Lisa Papademetriou**, a Texan by birth . . . **Sophie Masson**, born in Indonesia, brought up in France and Australia . . . **Elizabeth E. Wein**, born in New York City, brought up in England and Jamaica, now living in Scotland . . . **Susan Juby** from Canada . . . **Susan Vaught** from Tennessee . . . **O. R. Melling**, born in Ireland, raised in Canada, now back home in Ireland . . . **Zu Vincent and Kiara Koenig**, two American authors from the West Coast.

Read their biographies at the end of each article. You could hardly find a more diverse bunch in terms of background, interests, and achievements, but I can confidently predict they all share several things in common:

- They all know that magic moment when a window opens up on the word-processor page and allows them to step through into a different world.

- They all meet with spirit creatures (commonly called "characters") who live, laugh, love, and weep quite independently of the authors who call them up.

- They all recognize plots as fey and fragile things that may work out as planned . . . or take turns the writer never dreamed of.

- They all pray for those golden days when they don't have to write a word of their own, but take dictation from their Muse instead, creating marvels in the process.

Because they all share these experiences, they bring a special insight—something far beyond mere literary criticism—into the works of another of their kind. And this is especially true when the works in question enchanted them as children.

You may remember the moment yourself, perhaps at Christmas or a birthday, when you opened the package and found yourself staring at a brand-new, lovely book with all its new-book feel and smell. Except it wasn't a book, not like the books you'd read before. It was a doorway to another reality.

Can you remember how you stepped through that doorway somewhere on the second page? How your worries—the neglected homework, the cross father, the sick hamster—simply faded away? How you met new friends and visited strange lands? How you *became* the hero of the book?

Very few people realize it, but reading fiction is an *interactive* experience. The author of the novel does scarcely half the job. You, as the reader, do the rest, painting background scenery with your imagination, filling in the color of the dragon's eyes, listening to the whisper of the wind, reading the villain's darkest thoughts. This is a magical process by any rational definition of the term. It involves illusion, creation, healing, transports of delight, silent sounds heard only with the inner ear, impossible sights, wonders, marvels, conjurations.

And the magic reached its peak the day you entered Narnia.

It doesn't always happen, and regrettably it doesn't happen often, but sometimes an author crafts a work of such consummate skill that it carries you off to an enchanted realm you will remember to your dying day.

I'm betting your first C. S. Lewis book was *The Lion, the Witch and the Wardrobe,* but if I'm wrong, it doesn't matter. Narnia became a living place in Lewis's mind and he managed, in his writing, to open up a portal so you could come and share it, too. He did this partly by his writing skills, but mainly through his novel's themes. Narnia is mythic in the true sense of that word, a realm of wonder where humanity's great stories can be acted out—the sacrifice of heroes, the war of Light and Darkness, the triumph of Good over Evil, the initiation of youth, the wisdom of age, betrayal and hope, but above all, love.

These are things that touch us to the deepest levels of our souls and these are the themes of Narnia. When stuffy academics discuss the influence religion had on Lewis, they talk of something profoundly unimportant. It was not his Christianity that counted, but his archetypal, mythic spirituality that enabled him to reach out across every culture and creed to the children of the world.

A few of the children he reached were a little different from the others—introverted, perhaps, prone to daydreams, sometimes solitary, emotional, and difficult. Such children were swallowed up by Narnia. They found themselves in a place they could describe *completely*, far beyond the words that Lewis wrote. They found themselves in conversations with the Lion and the Faun that never appeared on the printed page. These were children with a special destiny—to create worlds of their own and let you share them.

Many factors led to the unfolding of that special destiny. We might speculate about parental support, or lack of it, about personal tragedy, meetings with remarkable men and women, encouragement, discouragement, discovery of creative wellsprings, travel, opportunity, or just dumb luck. But behind the diverse paths there was always that turning point, that tipping point, that trigger, in the moment when, as children, they opened their special book, visited Narnia and were themselves enchanted.

Thus the anthology you hold is something wonderful. It is the work of authors who have, one and all, fallen desperately in love with Narnia, the luminous creation of C. S. Lewis. And it is the work of authors who understand exactly what he went through to bring it into being.

Read and enjoy.

Herbie Brennan
New Year's Day, 2008

This is where the enchantment began for so many of us. Deb Caletti has produced a richly evocative recollection of her first trip to Narnia, carried there by the set of books she received from her parents for Christmas when she was only ten years old, and describes how the magic was passed on when she had children of her own. . . .

◄┼►◄※►◄┼►

Just Another Crazed Narnia Fan

Deb Caletti

When I was in the sixth grade, I loaned my copy of *The Lion, the Witch and the Wardrobe* to Lisa Miller and never got it back.

Not that I hold a grudge.

Lisa had a surgery that required breaking both her legs and resetting them, putting her in a wheelchair for the good part of a year. Flimsy excuse, yes? I mean, this was my beloved and cherished copy, part of the ENTIRE SET of the Chronicles of Narnia that my parents had given me for Christmas when I was ten. An entire set of Narnia books without *The Lion, the Witch and the Wardrobe*—it's like an entire set of dishes without the, well, *dishes*.

I still remember getting those books. For some reason, my mother had hidden them, unwrapped, inside a set of decorative drums that were underneath the Christmas tree. One day I was messing around, as any proper ten-year-old will do, and I opened up the drums. I was shocked, thrilled, surprised, and guilt-ridden at accidentally finding my gift. I knew they were meant to be mine. They had to be. First of all, I was the resident inhaler of books, bringing home stacks of them from the library that I'd consume same as popcorn before the movie even started. Second, they were meant to be mine because they just *had* to be mine. The covers alone told me so—that castle and the crazed-haired witch; that prince against the orange background, sword drawn against his chest; that magical boat. . . .

Knowing the books were there but being unable to have them yet—it was as if I loved chocolate and was forced to go into See's Candies with no money and my hands tied behind my back. They waited enticingly, and then, finally, they were mine. There is a hideous Christmas photo from that time—I am in tangled hair and wearing a white nightgown, sitting in front of a purple bike with a banana seat. But it is the books that are on my lap, that my fingertips are touching.

And so, like millions of children around the world, I entered the wardrobe. And once through, I discovered a wondrous land of creatures and adventures and powerful feelings. Ogres and Fauns and frozen places beginning to thaw. Unspeakable evil and goodness so good it brought you to tears. Battles and magic and vials of potions that cured every ill. I wanted to keep pushing through those coats until I reached that place, until I heard the snow crunch underfoot, felt the chill wind, saw the yellow glow of what might have been a lamppost off in the distance.

I read the books out of order, and so my first trip to Narnia was the same as Lucy's. And, same as Lucy, I would want to tell the others about my trip, all others, but no one would quite believe me until they had experienced it themselves. In addition to thrusting the books on friends, I tried to express my experience through my own writing—a story I wrote when I was twelve should have been named "The Voyage of the Something That Isn't the Dawn Treader but May as Well Be the Dawn Treader." It was the tale of a trip to a land with Talking Animals, and proved without question that one could overuse the word "mysterious."

I revisited Narnia, finding other ways to enter—through a painting on a wall, a magic ring, the Wood between the Worlds. I grew up in the suburbs of California, during the time the "mod" color for appliances was olive green. We had sidewalks and a community pool where you were required to wear a bathing cap. But I disappeared into the eaves of old houses, into an ocean of flowers and islands of dreams, into a land where a great Lion breathed life into animals so that they might speak. In real life, I fought off mean boys who snapped your new bra and smacked you with the small red rubber ball during dodge ball, struggled with my inabilities to do all the things girls seemed to know how to do—spin circles on the bars, lift a cat's cradle from the fingers of your best friend, chase Larry Hogan, the cute boy. But in Narnia, you could be small and be heroic. Mean boys got what was coming to them. Hurt bodies and hearts were made new. The worst kind of evil, a sledge speeding through snow— even it would stop when spring was allowed back again.

My Narnia love did not stop when I supposedly "grew up." A fine thing happened, which is that I had children. A fine thing in any case, but an added bonus when they were old enough to sit through a reading aloud, at Christmastime, of *The Lion, the Witch and the Wardrobe.* All of the expected and great things happened: they listened with wide eyes and begged for more. They cried when Aslan—well, you know—and I grabbed their pajama sleeves and said, "Wait, wait. Don't worry, you'll see!" It was as satisfying a reading experience as you could get, so much so that we repeated it the next year, and the next, and I confess here that (as a Narnia fan will do) I carried things a bit too far. I understand, I do, that people who have lockers and are old enough to get their driver's permits don't want to sit with their mother on the couch and hear a story they've heard a million times, even if she does beg and nearly cry and say, "Pleeeeeeeze!" My children, bless them, as *they* will do, held their ground, and found other ways through the years to indulge the Narnia fan that made their lunches. They bought me an ENTIRE SET of Narnia books, complete and whole, finally. They took me to *The Lion, the Witch and the Wardrobe* when the film was released, and my son put together a gift from a San Francisco bookstore for me—a gorgeous, life-sized cardboard wardrobe that was a promotional piece for the film, a wardrobe of endless sections and tabs and slots but with doors that opened and displayed a snowy land and a lamppost that really lights up. He had to cut the bottom off of it to even get it to fit into my office. My kids also participated in a Turkish Delight taste test in our London hotel room. A disappointing affair, I might add. After imagining for years its buttery and mouth-watering perfection, delectable enough to make a boy turn traitor against his own siblings, I was rather let down to find it was actually something you'd want to spit into a napkin.

This is my own story of Narnia love, and it is only one story of eighty-five million others. *Eighty-five million!* That's how many books have been sold, anyway, of the seven volumes that make up the Chronicles of Narnia, outsold only by Harry Potter. Eighty-five million—that's roughly the population of France and Sweden and Switzerland combined, plus a smaller country of your choice. Narnia has an obvious lasting appeal and a devoted following. Devoted, hmm. Crazed might be more accurate. Merely type the word "Narnia" into Google's narrow rectangle, and a treasure of 12,300,000 hits will pour down upon you like a trove of pirate riches.

Numbers are only part of the picture, though, because devotion, being devotion, generally has no finite number attached. A look at the variety of offerings on the Web gives you an idea of just how hard these books have hit our collective consciousness. Sure, there are book and movie reviews, articles, and products. Amazon alone offers some 4,000 Narnia-related goods for sale, from Sir Peter's knight shield (very cool), to bookends (have those), to an Aslan marionette (thin, lame, and frankly, a bit strange), to Divan Turkish Delight with Pistachio (I've already warned you). And there are plenty of guidebooks and maps, should you make a wrong turn at the lamppost. But what's most fascinating is the glimpse beyond the consumer harvest, to Narnia fandom at its most pure.

Think of this—you've got busy people here (I assume busy, at least busy in that they must make a living and take care of children and remember to let the dog out and go to the bank). And yet you see the countless hours involved in the numerous Narnia fan sites, countless spent—not only by the people who create and maintain these sites, but those who visit and contribute. There are reading groups, writing groups, Narnia-related costume parties. Crafts, decorating ideas (my kids would have me committed if I made that bed canopy). There are on-going lectures and a C. S. Lewis Society (general membership is twenty-five bucks), artists whose life works are based on Narnia scenes, as well as fiction, films, and music created by fans. There's a Swedish Christian metal band by the name of Narnia, as well as many businesses with its name—a pet-training company, a florist, a kennel. Various vacation spots—cabins and hideaways and tranquil settings suitable for weddings and other special occasions. There are sites where visitors display the Narnia costumes they've made and designed, and a Narnia Museum in Wheaton, Illinois, which holds C. S. Lewis's own boyhood wardrobe, along with his family memorabilia, photos, letters, and more. Five thousand people a year visit.

You can, if you're inclined, participate in forums on fan sites, tell Narnia jokes, take a Narnia Personality Test. Answer questions like, "Would you consider yourself brave?" (responses from "Quite Timid" to "Very"), and "Be honest, are you at all gullible?" and find out if you're a White Witch or an Edmund, or, as I learned, a Mr. Beaver ("Despite your size, as Mr. Beaver, you are decisive, confident and bold. You are brave in times of need and show great loyalty to those you respect").[1]

You wonder if poor old C. S. Lewis, taking that life-altering walk in the woods with Tolkien (the walk that, legend has it, held the seeds to the Chronicles), could have ever imagined *this*.

And, too, you wonder *why*. Why have these books with these characters hit us with such force? When a book generally

---

[1] Narniaquiz.com, a division of Narniaweb.com.

stays on a shelf for no more than three or four months, why have these particular books continued to weave themselves so permanently and powerfully into our lives and hearts?

I understand that for many the answer to that question involves the elements of the books that are their controversial backbone—the Christian parallels. Or, as the headline in an article in the *Sunday Times* succinctly put it, "The Narnia Lion Really Is Jesus." Reading the books as a child, though, I was clueless to this aspect of them, and it was only when I read *The Lion, the Witch and the Wardrobe* as an adult that I went, "Hmm. This reminds me of . . . Oh." Critics of the book's message will say that this cluelessness doesn't impair Lewis from achieving his goal—unwitting readers will still suck up that message same as hidden phrases in record album lyrics or buried images in advertising. Proponents of the books' message will *also* say that this cluelessness doesn't impair Lewis from achieving his goal. Religious educators use the books outright to nudge children toward their own objectives.

For me, though, and I think for many, the real, lasting appeal of the books is far simpler and more pure than the tangled motivations of religious or secular belief. The reasons for their timelessness are more straightforward and rare than religious fervor, though some would say worthy, too, of adulation—great storytelling, beautiful language. Like all good books, the magic is in the word choice, the rhythms; in the story, in the setting, in the characters. Less "The Lion Is Really Jesus" and more "The Lion Is So Magnificent, You Too Would Give Anything to Ride on His Back." The characters speak to our painful and victorious experiences of childhood in safe ways: the White Witch is that cruel teacher at the blackboard,

who gives homework over winter break; maybe even a parent
whose slap of a hand can sound like that whip. Edmund Pevensie and Eustace Scrubb—they're the bad boys who teased you
about your braces or who stepped on the back of your shoe to
make you trip. Tumnus, who didn't get it right at first, but tried
again and did it better—he's you, and so are Peter and Susan,
the brave and kind and solid boy or girl you try to be when
you raise your hand politely and stand in line without causing trouble. It's that moment in *The Wizard of Oz*, when Dorothy returns home and sees the characters in her dream world
in her real life—the scarecrow is the farm hand, the witch is
Dorothy's wicked neighbor. We understand the characters of
Narnia—as children, especially, we understand them—their
struggles over bad things, the struggle to be heard. The need
to believe in one all-powerful being, who will finally arrive and
set things right.

And story. Good versus evil, what larger story than that? A
saga that's close to our hearts at any age. We know that need,
we *live* that need, to triumph over things bigger than ourselves,
whether it be a raging father or a bad windstorm, a friend who
you told your secrets to and who betrayed you, or the time you,
too, felt like you'd been turned to stone. When we read the
Chronicles of Narnia, we are masters over all those things and
bigger things still. We are masters over Dwarfs and Dryads and
spells and even death. We carry swords and are brave.

And we do it in a magical setting. There are no mini-marts
here, or traffic jams. No loud mall music or parking lots littered
with cigarette stubs. No toxic waste dumps or hulking Costco
buildings with soy sauce bottles bigger than your head. No
sounds of clanging shopping carts or sirens, or the thumping

bass from a jacked-up truck. Here, in Narnia, the land is lush and fanciful. There are patches of warm sunlight and cool green thickets and wide mossy glades. There is an Arthurian stone table, and a castle with a beautiful name, Cair Paravel. There are the Wild Lands of the North and the Great Forest. It is "always winter and never Christmas" and then snow turns to slush and the green tips of flowers poke through the once-solid mass of white.

But finally, there is language. To me, the true origins of the power of Narnia can be found here—in the tender word choice and lulling rhythms of these works.

This, from when Lucy enters the wardrobe in *The Lion, the Witch and the Wardrobe*:

> And then she saw that there was a light ahead of her; not a few inches away where the back of the wardrobe ought to have been, but a long way off. Something cold and soft was falling on her. A moment later she found that she was standing in the middle of a wood at night-time with snow under her feet and snowflakes falling through the air.

And this, in the same book, when Lucy and Susan are riding Aslan:

> Have you ever had a gallop on a horse? Think of that; and then take away the heavy noise of the hoofs and the jingle of the bits and imagine instead the almost noiseless padding of the great paws. Then imagine instead of the black or grey or chestnut back of the horse the soft roughness of golden fur, and the mane flying back in the wind.

Simple words. Snow under feet. Noiseless padding of great paws. Words with imagery both gentle and sturdy, fanciful and yet everyday. Here, I believe, is where the enduring essence and the real magic lie. In these simple, simple words, these potent pictures of sensory detail, these delicate and sparse but impossibly rich sentences. Evocative words, dreamy even. And yet solid and tangible. The word choice is Hemingway-esque: physical, solid, present, yet somehow wistful and suggestive. Add magic and childhood, and suddenly you're a step beyond the enduring devotion of Hemingway fans into the crazy, boundless territory of Sir Peter desktop statues and Cair Paravel welcome mats. The enchantment is easy to understand, I think. The words we all know, laced with what we can only imagine.

My Narnia love will be one of those lasting pieces of me, I realize. The characters in my books often love Narnia as I do, and the idea of walking through a wardrobe and feeling your presence there so strongly that you see your own breath is an image I often share with other writers about the writing process itself. My love for the books stays as pure and simple as the language that created them.

And although I will pass on the Narnia fleece throw, the Aslan pocket watch, and the Lucy's Vial pewter necklace, and will forego the annual C. S. Lewis Conference and forum discussions on Narnia and faith—Lisa Miller, from Mr. Deebach's class at Ben Franklin Elementary? If you're out there somewhere? I'd still like that book back.

——◄►◄◄◄►◄►◄——

Deb Caletti is a National Book Award Finalist whose books are published and translated worldwide. In addition to other distinguished recognition, Deb has also been a PEN USA Literary Award finalist, and has received the Washington State Book Award. Her novels include *The Queen of Everything*; *Honey, Baby, Sweetheart*; *The Nature of Jade*; and *The Secret Life of Prince Charming*, among others. Her seventh book with Simon & Schuster, *Stay*, will be released in 2011. Paul G. Allen's Vulcan Productions (*Hard Candy*, *Far From Heaven*) and Foundation Features (*Capote*, *Stone of Destiny*) have also partnered to develop Deb's novels into a film series titled *Nine Mile Falls*. She lives with her family in Seattle.

Sometimes the most important things are hidden in plain sight—under your nose, or under your feet. Brent Hartinger thinks that's the most important message C. S. Lewis hid in Narnia. Hartinger explains how he found magic—real magic—in his own life by listening to that message . . . and how you can do the same.

◄►◄►❋◄►◄►

Forgotten Castles and Magical Creatures in Hiding

On Seeing Hidden Things in *Prince Caspian*

BRENT HARTINGER

A wild forest grew across the street from the house in the suburbs where I grew up. Technically, it was merely a "holding basin"—a patch of land that city engineers had set aside from development to hold back the floodwaters that occasionally swelled up from the little creek that ran through the neighborhood. But it was dense and untamed; much of it was swampland, which made it inaccessible to all but those with a strong sense of adventure, not to mention hip-boots.

As a boy, my friends and I spent almost every waking hour in that forest, and slowly but surely it surrendered its secrets: a broken well, a decaying shack left by homesteaders, part of

an abandoned railroad track said to have been laid over an old
Indian trail. Once, while walking through dense thicket in the
fall, my friends and I noticed that many of the trees were suddenly sporting big red apples, crisp and delicious. *Oh!* we realized. *Orchard Street got its name because it ran along an* actual
orchard!

All this in an area not even a square mile in size.

I can't help think about that little wood whenever I re-read
Prince Caspian. Upon first inspection, the forest in which Peter,
Susan, Edmund, and Lucy find themselves after being drawn to
Narnia from the English train station is dense and impenetrable,
too. Even after fighting their way out of a thicket of thorns and
nettles, they're somewhere completely unfamiliar.

At first they wonder, is it even Narnia? "It might be any-
where," says Peter.

But then they begin exploring the area, and slowly but
surely, this new place—an island, it seems—gives up its secrets.
First they too find an orchard, overgrown amid the brambles.

"Then this was once an inhabited island," Peter concludes.

Next they find an old stone wall, and a stone arch—ruins
that were once a castle.

"Ages ago, by the looks of it," says Edmund.

In other words, they've found a *forgotten* castle, and a surprisingly familiar one at that. "How it all comes back!" Lucy
says, remembering their own castle from their previous visit to
Narnia, when they ruled as kings and queens. "We could pretend we were in Cair Paravel now."

But then they find a chess piece they recognize, and Peter
comes to a sudden realization: the ruins of this forgotten castle
are, in fact, the ruins of Cair Paravel. They've returned to Narnia

after all, but in a different time period, hundreds, or perhaps thousands, of years in the future.

The secret of this forest is revealed at last. It starts out, upon their arrival, being "so thick and tangled that they could hardly see into it at all." But then that which is hidden is revealed, and they learn they are in the most familiar place there is: home.

Prince Caspian is a novel of hidden things. Unlike in the other books in the Narnia series, castles and magic are not immediately evident. For the first five (of fifteen) chapters, there are no Fauns with parasols or beautiful Witches with enchanted Turkish Delight. Not only do the Narnian animals not talk, they don't even seem to exist: in the island forest where Peter and the others find themselves, "nothing in it moved—not a bird, not even an insect." Even the ghosts of these Black Woods turn out to have been fabricated by the Telmarines to keep people away.

Indeed, for both the Pevensies and for Prince Caspian himself, the Narnia of the early *Prince Caspian* chapters appears, at least at first blush, to be a lot like the "real" world: nondescript and ordinary—perhaps even more so than the *real* "real" world of England at the beginning of *The Magician's Nephew*, which at least includes humming magic teleportation rings in its first chapter.

But eventually hidden things are revealed in *Prince Caspian*, just as they were in that little forest of my suburban childhood: brambles become ruins that become castles, even familiar ones. There *are* extraordinary things in the Narnia of *Prince Caspian*— they're just not so obvious. They're only available to those who take the time to go exploring, and those who are willing to set preconceptions aside and really *look*.

And then there's the magic.

In *The Magician's Nephew*, we learn of Narnia's beginning, and the fact that it is literally founded by magic; Aslan's magic permeates the land down to its very soil, which even has the power, at least at first, to grow lampposts and toffee trees. While Narnian magic fades somewhat in the "real" world of England, a bite of a Narnian apple is still enough to cure the deadliest of diseases.

In *Prince Caspian* we learn that, for the first (and only) time in Narnian history, the forces of non-magic—the forces of the ordinary—have invaded and conquered Narnia. Miraz has become "Lord Protector," protecting the occupiers of the land not from further invasions, but from the truth about the country's mystical past. In all the years of Narnia's existence, Miraz is the only one to succeed in subverting the land's essentially magical nature. In *The Horse and His Boy*, we learn that Calormen fear Narnian magic, but even they fail in their one disastrous invasion attempt. And while the White Witch might be Narnia's most persistent foe, even she never destroys or suppresses its magical underpinnings; she merely wants to replace its good magic with her own evil stuff—hers is a *magical* eternal winter, after all.

But by the time Caspian is born, Narnia seems to be a land devoid of magic. That said, Prince Caspian hears tales of "Old Narnia" from Nurse and desperately wants to believe:

> He dreamed of Dwarfs and Dryads every night and tried very hard to make the dogs and cats in the castle talk to him. But the dogs only wagged their tails and the cats only purred.

Miraz, of course, forbids all discussion of magic—even any "thinking" of it. And for breaching the protocol with Caspian, Nurse is summarily dismissed. But the essential nature of anything cannot be suppressed forever, and it's not long before Caspian's new tutor, Doctor Cornelius, hints at the truth to Nurse's stories. Eventually, Doctor Cornelius tells Caspian all—but only at the top of a tall, locked tower in the dead of night.

"All you have heard about Old Narnia is true," Doctor Cornelius says.

But the question on Caspian's lips is: might the magical creatures of Old Narnia still be out there somewhere in hiding?

> "I don't know—I don't know," said the Doctor with a deep sigh.
>
> "Sometimes I am afraid there can't be. I have been looking for traces of them all my life. Sometimes I have thought I heard a Dwarf-drum in the mountains. Sometimes at night in the woods, I thought I had a glimpse of Fauns and Satyrs dancing a long way off; but when I came to the place, there was never anything there."

For me, these images are the most indelible in the whole book, and possibly in the entire Narnia series; they're definitely the most relevant to my own life. Fading Dwarf-drums and dancing Fauns and Satyrs glimpsed from a distance but gone without a trace when an attempt is made to confirm their existence? In a few sentences, C. S. Lewis perfectly captured what is so tantalizing about hidden and forgotten things, especially magical ones: the fact that what we can't see might be so much more spectacular than what we can, that what we've forgotten might be far better than what still is.

Let's face it: the ordinary world can be pretty crappy, both in the aftermath of World War II, when Lewis was writing the Chronicles of Narnia, and now, in our era of corporate and religious terrorism, not to mention global warming. In *Prince Caspian*, Lewis got right to the heart of our human desire for more than this, for a hope in something better. It's not for nothing that we humans—some of us, anyway—are always heading off across unexplored oceans and empty expanses of space, or at least gathering around televisions and hurrying to bookstores and movie theaters in order to experience the latest transformative story like that of the Chronicles of Narnia.

And yet, these images of Doctor Cornelius's fruitless searches also include the deep wariness with which most of us approach the search for that which is hidden: the very real fear of disappointment. I at least remember all too well my disillusionment when I learned that Santa wasn't "real," that I'd been lied to all along, seemingly for the amusement of adults. I can still recall the sting of my reluctant adolescent realization that I couldn't play Jedi mind tricks or lift objects with the power of the Force. And I'll never forget my weary acceptance of the fact that the Patterson Bigfoot film was faked and that there simply aren't enough fish in Loch Ness to sustain a breeding population of anything resembling a monster.

I for one have definitely experienced Doctor Cornelius's deep sigh of disappointment.

I guess it was all just in my imagination.

In short, the danger in searching for hidden things is that we risk not finding them.

Of course, magical creatures do exist in *Prince Caspian*'s Narnia, in *hiding*. In chapter six, entitled "The People Who Lived in Hiding," Caspian finally meets them firsthand: the Dwarfs, the Three Bulgy Bears, Glenstorm the Centaur, Reepicheep the Mouse, and all the rest.

Better still, he has proof he isn't imaging things:

> When Caspian woke the next morning, he could
> hardly believe it that it had all been a dream; but the
> grass was covered with little cloven hoof marks.

Suddenly it's Doctor Cornelius's endless searching but with a different ending: the Dwarfs have beat their drums, and the Fauns have danced, but this time they've left behind *footprints*—telltale signs of their existence! The People Who Lived in Hiding have come into the open at last. At this point, the war between Mirez and Old Narnia is inevitable; after all, the world of the ordinary and the world of magic cannot coexist.

Like Doctor Cornelius, I've spent a lot of my life looking for hidden things. But even as a kid, I wasn't content merely with forgotten castles—the old train tracks and abandoned orchards of that forest near my house. After reading books like the Chronicles of Narnia, I wanted *magic*.

I did find plenty of creatures in hiding. That forest was literally teeming with wildlife. There were foxes and deer and bats and raccoons in the trees, snakes and frogs and turtles and ducks in the swamp, eels and crawdads and trout and salmon in the stream.

The adults in my neighborhood ignored all this or, like Miraz, seemed actively hostile to the idea of wildlife hiding in their midst. In the 1970s there was barely a concept of organic gardening or polluted run-off, at least in my hometown. I remember walking once at night along a row of houses that lined an area of swamp. Almost every one of them had a "bug-zapper" out back—a humming machine that attracted insects with its light, then zapped them with electricity when they got too close. The night was filled with little snaps and pops as these machines electrocuted insects by the thousands. Did they honestly think they could build a house on a swamp, then somehow drain it of its insects?

Actually, they did, and could. As the years went by, my childhood friends and I all noticed the waning of the wildlife. Thirty years later, that holding basin still exists, but it's now almost completely devoid of life, a slimy, silent place with a foul smell. Just like the world of magic and the world of the ordinary cannot coexist, apparently wilderness and civilization can't coexist for long, either. Even that little patch of Eden was too much for most to bear.

All these hidden animals my friends and I were finding at the time? They definitely weren't "ordinary," but they weren't The People Who Lived in Hiding, either. If they were too magical for the neighbors with perfectly manicured lawns, they weren't magical enough for me. I wanted Dwarfs and Fairies and Dryads and Centaurs. Like Caspian, I wanted my animals to talk!

So I kept looking. Like Doctor Cornelius, I often saw glimpses of things that looked promising. Once I saw a strange orange light flickering just over the horizon. I walked for an hour only to discover that it was merely the burning off of methane from a nearby garbage dump.

I didn't give up. I kept searching. Magic—I was *determined* to find it!

And eventually I did.

◆❈◆❈◆

It's true that the castles and magical creatures in *Prince Caspian*'s Narnia are hidden from view, but the biggest obstacles to seeing them aren't the brambles that grew up around them or the mountain trees that obscured them. They're the observer's own self-limitations, their inability to see beyond the ordinary.

In other words, seeing hidden things is mostly a question of perception.

We see the first example of this when the Pevensies are sorting out the secret of Cair Paravel. "It's about time we four starting using our brains," Peter says. And Lucy, keenly attuned to the world of magic, answers, "I've felt for hours that there was some wonderful mystery hanging over this place."

Then Peter lays out the pieces of the puzzle: the orchard planted by Lilygloves the Mole, the size and shape of the ruined hall, the chess piece, and—the final confirmation—the door to the treasure room, exactly where it should be, though covered by a curtain of ivy.

This isn't a forgotten castle, at least not anymore; now its identity is obvious. The Pevensies merely needed to change their perspectives—a change that comes for all of them in a moment of *gestalt*, that time of sudden realization when all the little details of something come together into a unified whole, and a person sees "the big picture" for the first time.

When Doctor Cornelius tells Caspian of Old Narnia, the prince has his own moment of gestalt:

> All at once Caspian realized the truth and felt that
> he ought to have realized it long before. Doctor Cor-
> nelius was so small, and so fat, and had such a very
> long beard. Two thoughts came into his head at the
> same moment. One was a thought of terror—"He's
> not a real man, he's a *Dwarf*, and he's brought me up
> here to kill me." The other was sheer delight—"There
> are real Dwarfs still, and I've seen one at last."

When it comes to magical creatures in hiding, there was one hiding right in front of Caspian all along. But until Caspian changed his perspective, he had no chance of seeing him.

Magic, it seems, is sometimes hard to see, even in Narnia.

Indeed, when extraordinary (but hidden) things are finally revealed, there will always be those who simply choose not to see them, or who are unable to handle their existence. According to Lewis, that might even be *most* humans. Right before the final defeat of the Telmarines by Old Narnia, Aslan travels the land restoring its magic and beauty. This presents a problem for Miss Prizzle, the Telmarine schoolmarm whose classroom has suddenly been transformed into a forest:

> Miss Prizzle found she was standing on grass in
> a forest glade. She clutched at her desk to steady
> herself, and found that the desk was a rose-bush.
> Wild people such as she had never even imagined
> were crowding round her. Then she saw the Lion,
> screamed and fled, and with her fled her class, who
> were mostly dumpy, prim little girls with fat legs.

Miss Prizzle had never even *imagined* such creatures? Well, that's her problem right there; to paraphrase Yoda, *that* is why she fails. If there's never been any room in her world-view for the extraordinary, if she can't even *imagine* them, why would she be able to perceive them when confronted by them in real life?

And then there's the curious question of seeing Aslan himself, the most magical of all Narnia's creatures, but also—at least at times—one of its best hidden.

When the Pevensies and Trumpkin travel from Cair Paravel to join Caspian at Aslan's How, they're not sure of the quickest path, and Aslan appears to lead the way. Naturally, Lucy, with her wide-open mind, is quick to spot him.

But the others *don't* see, and—except for Edmund—they don't believe that Lucy does either. After a vote, they choose not to follow Aslan's lead. Before long, they naturally find themselves at a dead end.

That night, Lucy wakes to find that not only can she see Aslan, she can see the sleeping spirits of the Narnian trees waking at last. Aslan directs her to get the others, which she tries to do; Edmund is the only sibling she's able to wake, and he's still unable to see Aslan. "There's nothing there," he says to Lucy. "You've got dazzled and muddled with the moonlight. One does, you know. I thought I saw something for a moment myself. It's only an optical what-do-you-call-it."

Edmund isn't able to see the Lion because he hasn't yet had a change in perception, the Aslan-related moment of gestalt.

Edmund does see him eventually—first Aslan's shadow, then the Lion himself. Shortly thereafter, Peter sees him too.

Close-minded Susan, the one who spitefully encourages the others to ignore Lucy's pleadings, is the last Pevensie to be able to see Aslan. But finally even she sees what was so obvious to Lucy all along. She apologizes to Lucy for not believing her, saying, "But I've been far worse than you know. I really believed it was him—he, I mean . . . I mean, deep down inside. Or I could have, if I'd let myself."

Susan *could have* seen the Lion if she'd let herself—if she'd previously exercised the muscles of her imagination, and if she'd opened her mind enough to consider the possibility of the unexpected.

Problem is, she didn't.

━━◄►◄※►◄►━━

What magic did I find in that little forest by the house of my suburban childhood? Like the Pevensies and the ruins of Cair Paravel, and like Prince Caspian and Doctor Cornelius, it wasn't anything that hadn't been right in front of me all along.

I just needed a change in my perspective.

For example, one afternoon my friends and I put on our boots and headed out across Mud Island, this flat expanse of mud in the middle of the swamp. But the mud was deeper than we'd expected, and I'd barely gotten five feet when my walking stick got stuck in the muck (not to mention my boots). I had no choice but to leave the stick behind (not to mention my boots). My walking stick remained there, standing upright in the mud.

A few weeks later, I noticed leaves sprouting from the top of that stick. It had taken root in the rich, wet muck of Mud Island.

By the following year it had turned into a small tree. I proudly watched that tree grow for the rest of my childhood. Before long, it was a massive alder that towered over the whole island.

Okay, so it wasn't exactly a toffee tree growing from a piece of candy, or a lamppost taking root in the ground. But, hey, toffee trees don't grow even in Narnia, not after the first few days of its existence, after Aslan's initial burst of creation magic fades. That tree I inadvertently planted on Mud Island was pretty magical.

As for animals that talk, I once spent half an hour watching a family of foxes in that forest. Initially, they were frightened of me. But when it became clear that I was no danger, that I was merely sitting in the grass and watching from afar, they began to relax. The kits began to play with each other while the mother kept a wary eye on me. Don't tell me she wasn't communicating to me loudly and clearly.

And what of the river gods and Dryads and the rest of the forest spirits? Well, I've still never actually seen one, but I've definitely felt *something* in those woods. When the day comes that we learn trees have an intelligence of sorts, I won't be surprised in the least.

So magic is hidden all around us, visible if we're simply willing to open our eyes? And the line between imagination and reality isn't nearly as strong as some would like us to believe? Is that what I'm saying?

Well, yes, that's pretty much it. But it's not just me. I happen to think it's exactly what C. S. Lewis was saying with the entire Chronicles of Narnia series, and I think he came out and said it most directly in *Prince Caspian*.

Oh, not that trite old insight! you might be saying. *That's not real magic! That's not the way it is for the Pevensies when they go to Narnia or for Caspian and Doctor Cornelius when they go searching for the People Who Live in Hiding! They find the real thing! The kind of magic you're talking about only exists in your imagination.*

Have it your way. But for the record? That's exactly what Susan and Miss Prizzle would say.

◆ ▸►❋◄◂ ◆

Brent Hartinger is a four-time Book Sense Pick and the author of many novels for young people, including *Geography Club* and his latest, *Shadow Walkers*, about astral projecting teens (coming in Winter 2011). Brent also edits the fantasy-themed website TheTorchOnline.com. Learn more at www.brenthartinger.com.

You know what they say: nice girls always seem to fall for the bad boys. But Diana Peterfreund explains how her crush on bad boy Edmund only really started when he began to see the error of his ways, and takes us on an extensive journey through the Chronicles of Narnia to illustrate the point that pure goodness can be . . . well . . . intimidating.

◆·▶◈◀·◆

King Edmund the Cute
Anatomy of a Girlhood Crush

DIANA PETERFREUND

Let's get it straight: I wasn't sitting around writing "Diana Hearts Edmund" in my Trapper Keeper, but I had an enormous crush on Edmund Pevensie when I was a kid. When I admit that to people, then and now, I invariably get a reaction that's halfway between bemused and appalled. *Edmund?* they say. *Isn't he the petulant, whiny traitor responsible for Aslan's death?*

Yes, yes he is. In *The Lion, the Witch and the Wardrobe*. But that's only the start of Edmund's adventures in Narnia. He pulls it together by the end of that book and proceeds to rock out for four more. No, Ed doesn't leave us with the best first impression in all of literature, but he more than makes up for it in the rest of the series.

If anything, his experiences in the first book[1] give him a breadth of knowledge and depth of experience and sorrow that surpass that of all the other children who become "friends of Narnia." C. S. Lewis *wants* Edmund to be one of the noblest characters in the series (barring Reepicheep, whom Lewis set up for sainthood from word one). He wants to show no mistake was too dire that you couldn't rise above it. And Edmund not only rises, he kicks butt . . . and I swoon.

But not at first.

When we meet Edmund, he's a cranky, spiteful little turd. His first act as a character is to ridicule his adorable kid sister about her Narnian "fantasies." Within a few pages, he's colluding with the White Witch in exchange for bon bons. Soon after, when Edmund lies to his siblings about visiting Narnia, Lewis describes it as "one of the nastiest things in this story." The death and dismemberment and turning of folks into stone? All pretty bad, but Edmund lying to his family and casting his lot with the Witch is the true betrayal here. When they speak of Edmund being a traitor, this is what they are talking about. He didn't turn against the Narnians, who were not—yet—his countrymen; he sold out his brother and sisters to the White Witch. He's already so far gone that by the time he hears Aslan's name

---

[1] *The Lion, the Witch and the Wardrobe.* I reject the new ordering system, whether or not it was the one Lewis supposedly favored. I think he was wrong, because *The Lion, the Witch and the Wardrobe* is an excellent intro to the world of Narnia, whereas *The Magician's Nephew* is a dark and dour book that gives away much of the plotline for all the books that come before it. I'm pleased to see that the movie makers have thus far agreed with me.

for the first time, from Mr. Beaver, he does not experience the delicious sensation the other children do. Instead, he feels only "mysterious horror."

Edmund's comeuppance arrives swiftly. He's barely at the Witch's castle before she shows her true colors, and his envy toward Peter begins to fade as he recognizes that maybe he was letting his bad attitude blind him toward the truth about that chick with the Turkish Delight and the wand. Edmund's turning point comes when the Witch takes out her frustration on a family of squirrels and he begs for their lives. She beats him, then says, "let that teach you to ask favor for spies and traitors," a statement that foreshadows her triumph when Aslan does the same on Edmund's behalf later on. Edmund's redemption has begun, however, for though he is half-frozen, starving, and lying in a bloody huddle at the back of the Witch's sledge, he, "for the first time in this story, felt sorry for someone besides himself."

Why I Heart Edmund

After Edmund admits his mistake, it's nothing but love, baby. When he is rescued from the Witch's clutches, the first thing that happens is a long and private (even from the reader) conversation with Aslan. It is one that Edmund never forgets, and it informs his character from that point on.

Later, he attempts to stop Aslan from striking the bargain with the White Witch, not knowing, as the Lion does, of the deeper magic that will ultimately redeem him. But more than anything, he saves all of Narnia in the final battle because Edmund alone figures out that the best way to defeat the Witch is to destroy the wand she's been using to turn her attackers into stone. When Lucy looks at him after the battle, she sees that the scars he's suffered at his "horrid" boarding school "where he had begun to go wrong" (all the Chronicles are concerned with the type of emotional abuse children receive at school) have faded away, and Edmund has "become his real old self again."

And he just gets better with age: "Edmund was a graver and quieter man than Peter, and great in council and judgment." It is this description of the adult King Edmund that abides throughout the rest of the series. Even when Edmund is once more transformed into a child, he remains a wise, thoughtful leader, and a shrewd and clever advisor. It is Edmund who comes up with the lion's share of plans in *Prince Caspian*: Edmund who first realizes how time moves differently in Narnia than in our world, Edmund who suggests dueling with the Dwarf Trumpkin to prove that they are worthy allies and Narnian royalty, and Edmund who devises the plan to meet Caspian at Aslan's How.

Nevertheless, he remembers his past and remains humbled by the experience. Though Lucy is the only one to see Aslan while they travel through the wilderness, Edmund still votes to follow her lead.

> When we first discovered Narnia a year ago—or a thousand years ago, whichever it was—it was Lucy who discovered it first and none of us would believe her. I was the worst of the lot, I know. Yet she was right after all. Wouldn't it be fair to believe her this time?

It was at that moment that I fell for Edmund, and fell hard, because, as all storytellers know, there is nothing more appealing than a bad guy gone good. Edmund knows where he's been, realizes how close he came to ruin, and wants above all to be worthy of the faith that Aslan and the Narnians have in him.

By the time Peter is writing the letter to Miraz, which describes his brother's full title: ". . . *our well-beloved and royal brother Edmund, sometime King under us in Narnia, Duke of Lantern Waste and Count of the Western March, Knight of the Noble Order of the Table*,"[2] my ten-year-old self was well and truly gone. (If I didn't write Countess of the Western March on my Trapper Keeper once or twice, I should have, because that's a very cool title to hold.) Edmund was my favorite character in the series (except for Reepicheep, as already stated, but he was a Mouse—can't have a literary crush on a Mouse).

Since the Narnian stories are, at their heart, redemption stories, Lewis includes in each a character whose fate it is to be redeemed by Narnian values, adventures, and faith. In *Prince Caspian*, the "cranky" and "disbeliever" mantles worn by Edmund in the first book are passed on to his sister Susan and Trumpkin, respectively. (Both, of course, get over it by the end of the book.) In the third book, *The Voyage of the Dawn Treader*, Lewis outdoes himself with the introduction of Eustace Clarence Scrubb.

Eustace, a cousin to the Pevensies, whines his way through the first half of the book. Like Edmund in *The Lion, the Witch and the Wardrobe*, he is suspicious and jealous of his companions, greedy for power and wealth, and cranky and selfish at every opportunity. But before he has the chance to cause any

---

[2] A designation that then and now makes me shiver. This, of course, is the knighthood that Aslan bestowed upon Edmund on the field of battle in *The Lion, the Witch and the Wardrobe*. Order of the *Table*? Talk about the potential for an endless guilt trip!

real damage, he's turned into a dragon. After Aslan feels the little snot has learned his lesson, he is restored to human form, and like Edmund, becomes a changed man. Naturally, the first person the penitent Eustace runs into is our darling Edmund, who alone among the denizens of the *Dawn Treader* can understand what it means to have your world rocked, Aslan-style. As he tells his cousin the story of his transformation and recovery, Eustace is by turns humble, contrite, and humiliated. When he apologies, Edmund responds: "Between ourselves, you haven't been as bad as I was on my first trip to Narnia. You were only an ass, but I was a traitor."

It's an important reminder. Because Eustace's beastliness goes on for the better half of the book—and is aimed against all of our old favorite characters: the Pevensies, Caspian, and darling, noble Reepicheep—we might forget that Edmund was way, *way* worse in his time. Remember how he was the reason Aslan *died*? Remember how he almost got his brother and sisters turned into stone? Huh? Remember?

And yet, for some reason, we just don't care. We're too much in *luuuv*. No matter how many great things Eustace does in subsequent books, I never fell for him. Maybe the problem is that *annoying* doesn't up your attractiveness quotient the same way *evil* does. Eustace was a pain in the butt, but Edmund was seriously dark. And every time he gets all noble and reminds us of his past, we love him even more for having the strength to overcome it.

Lewis can't resist showing us how much his atoning hero has grown, especially in the context of talking to characters who still have some growing to do. You never see Peter having these private moments with various newcomers. You never see King Caspian sitting around and talking about how deeply he understands someone else's moments of doubt. That one is all Edmund. And because Edmund cares, over and over, it's Edmund we care *about* as well.

"King Edmund the Just" continues the tradition he has become known for throughout the voyage: protecting his ship-mates from water that can turn you into gold, devising a strategy to deal with the Monopods, and demanding to know the truth about the enchanted sleepers (he even suspects that Ramandu's daughter is a witch, and Edmund knows from witches). And at the end of the voyage, when Aslan tells him he will never return to Narnia, it was the first time I ever cried for a fictional charac-ter.[3] I was heartbroken for Edmund, but also for myself. He and Lucy had been such a huge part of the series. How ever could I accept a Narnia book without them?

Which was why I was so thrilled to see them return when Lewis "flashed back" to the so-called Golden Age of Narnia in *A Horse and His Boy*. This grown-up King Edmund has yet to experience the adventures his boyhood self had in *Prince Caspian* and *The Voyage of the Dawn Treader*, and has, additionally, absorbed some strange, courtly, quasi-Medieval airs in his years ruling Narnia, but he is still the character we've grown to love.

Shasta, the hero of the novel, loves him on sight as well. As the Narnians parade through the Calormene streets, whistling and chatting and looking like the friendliest group of noblemen one could hope to meet, the young runaway sees for the first time the kind of people he wants to be. The Narnian royals are the cool kids in Tashbaan, and when Shasta is mistaken for one

---

[3] But far from the last. Curse you, *The Last Battle*!

of their ranks, he's alternately thrilled by their treatment (Soft cushions! Sherbets!) and terrified that they'll discover the truth.

So while Edmund does his "wise advisor" thing, plotting to save his increasingly silly sister Susan from the Calormene jerk courting her without causing a full-scale war between the nations, Shasta and the reader get ever more impressed by how kick-ass the grown-up Edmund is.[4] Still, we ain't seen nothing yet, as the King doesn't pull out all the stops until we reach the Fight at Anvard. In a series of breathless, long paragraphs narrated by the Hermit of the Southern March, we learn of Edmund's battlefield derring-do:

> King Edmund is dealing marvelous strokes. He's just slashed Corradin's head off. . . . King Edmund's down—no, he's up again: he's at it with Rabadash [Susan's would-be lover]. They're fighting in the very gate of the castle . . . Chlamash and Edmund are still fighting but the battle is over everywhere else. Chlamash has surrendered. The battle is over. The Calormenes are utterly defeated.

---

[4] Another argument (and honestly, I could make dozens) for why the books work better in the original order. If read in this order, the last time we see Susan before learning she is "no longer a friend of Narnia" since she's gotten too into fashions and dating and etc. (cf. *The Last Battle*) is here, where she is swooning and talking about courtiers and being timid and cowardly and in general not at all acting like the great archer she was in *The Lion, the Witch and the Wardrobe* or *Prince Caspian*. If read in the so-called "preferred" order, Susan whines here, gets it together in *Prince Caspian*, then disappears for two books before being shuffled right out of the series and denied entry into Narnian heaven. Reading *The Horse and His Boy* closer to *The Last Battle* does more to prepare us for this (as well as to prepare us for the heavy Calormene influence in the final installment).

Later we learn the details of how King Edmund bested Rabadash, which sadly was more due to the latter's own foolishness than any maneuver of our man. But still, you try leading an army into battle, beheading folks left and right!

What a thrilling moment that was for me as a reader! Peter, the wolf killer, the main fighter in the series, was out of town, and Edmund finally had a chance to lead his own battle and show that the whole thing with the Witch's wand hadn't been a fluke. It's very telling to me that when Lewis chose to write again about the Pevensies, the character he focused on was Edmund. Edmund— imperfect, redeemed, and eager to offset his mistakes—is a far more complex character than his ideal brother, his shallow sister Susan (who, curiously, has lost all her interest in archery in *The Horse and His Boy*), and the lighthearted but simple Lucy. Because we are also not perfect, it is Edmund we feel close to.

Edmund also displays what has become his most dominant character trait: his propensity for understanding and forgiveness of other characters. When Shasta reappears and apologizes to Edmund, swearing that he wasn't a traitor, the King is all too aware of the child's failings: "'I know now that you were no traitor, boy,' said King Edmund, laying his hand on Shasta's head." Compared to Edmund's own betrayal, Shasta's deeds didn't endanger anyone.[5] Later, he goes so far as to extend his compassion toward the cruel and cowardly Rabadash, saying, "'. . . even a traitor may mend. I have known one that did.' And he looked very thoughtful."

Edmund drops the "T" word a lot in *A Horse and His Boy*, possibly because penance and redemption are such strong

---

[5] He did come close, however, for Shasta had a moment or two back in the palace in Calormen where he half-hoped that Corin would never reappear and that he would be able to take the prince's place permanently.

themes throughout the novel. The traitorous Archenland knight who participated in Shasta's kidnapping is redeemed when he starves himself to keep the infant prince alive on the boat. Aravis is scratched by Aslan as penitence for the lashings received by her stepmother's slave as a result of Aravis's drugging. Even Bree has his saddle scared off for failing to trust in Aslan's Beast nature. And of course we have Rabadash's punishment. Lewis is really hammering home the idea, so of course he features Edmund, the poster boy for redemption.

The message is clear: Trust in Aslan and become a king. (Hey, it works for Shasta!) Edmund receives Aslan's forgiveness in *The Lion, the Witch and the Wardrobe*, and pays it forward to everyone he meets, from the accidentally dragon-ed to the orphan peasant boy, and finally, undeservedly, to the *villain of the novel*—who even Aslan decides is a real ass. Since we never get another scene from Ed's point of view, this is the closest you ever come to seeing his inner world after the events of *The Lion, the Witch and the Wardrobe*, and it hints at the way his personal history may have turned him into the "grave" king he becomes.

Still, though he always remembers the past, he doesn't wallow in it. Edmund isn't the type of guy to wander around his kingdom acting tortured. There are too many wars to fight, too many adventures to have, and most of all, too many people to guide along the path that he has already trod. Edmund is so happy in his skin that he prioritizes helping other people find their faith and inner strength. It's more valuable to take the experience—however awful—and grow from it than to let it warp your life. Lewis makes an important point with Edmund, and it was one I understood, even at ten.

Still, I wanted to give him a hug. Why aren't there any Narnian maidens around offering to give him one? Whither the Dryad looking to dance in Edmund's direction? After all, Susan and Lucy have a whole host of suitors after them, and the lords of every island the *Dawn Treader* visits throw their daughters at King Caspian. Even Shasta gets the girl at the end, when he grows up and marries the Tarkheena Aravis. But Edmund remains a free agent. No Countess of the Western March for him. And when I point this out to other fans of the series, they are always agog. *Why go after Edmund*, they argue, *when you could have the High King Peter*? Why make eyes at the legendary king from the past, when the *current* king was on the same ship?

Why indeed?

Edmund vs. the Other Narnian Men

1. PETER PEVENSIE

High King over All Kings of Narnia. Noble, Brave, Lion-Fearing, Possessed of a Magical Sword, Killer of Talking Wolves. Quite a list. A bit intimidating, actually. The problem with Peter as a crush object is that he's perfect. Even Edmund is intimidated by the nonstop faultlessness of his older brother. No doubt it is Peter's superiority in all things that accounts for Edmund's initial attitude problem. Can you imagine starting at a boy's school your flawless brother has already conquered? Edmund was probably treated like "the other Pevensie" all year long.

The only thing Peter does wrong in the entire series is to get lost in the woods even though Lucy asks him to follow her (which—ahem—*Edmund* wants to do without question). The other problem with Peter is that, given his sheer perfection, he doesn't have much of a personality. He's so smooth, so impeccable, that it's tough to get a handle on him. Where Edmund is logical, clever, understanding, damaged, grave, and quiet, Peter is just perfect. Perfect is *boring*.

2. KING CASPIAN

Sometimes called Caspian the Seafarer. The Boy King of Narnia is something of an adrenaline junkie, don't you think? Against the wishes of his advisors, who want him to stay home in his newly culturally blended kingdom, defend it from giants and Calormen, and get married, Caspian jets off to points unknown to find a bunch of old men who barely even deserved a mention in the previous book. And then, as if he hasn't gotten his way enough already, he decides that the whole king business is tired and that he wants to run off with Reepicheep to see the end of the world. (For my money, Caspian might have been much happier leaving the kingdom to his usurping uncle and tripping off to play Magellan. Tough luck for the Talking Beasts, though.) Indeed, during that little episode it's Edmund who yanks the petulant Caspian back from the brink (literally), even pulling rank, king-to-king, in order to make his point. I wonder if Ramandu's daughter would have been pleased to know how close Caspian came to abandoning her there on that island? She can take him!

3. EUSTACE CLARENCE SCRUBB

Please. I mean, he's a great kid and all, and he comports himself marvelously in *The Silver Chair*[6] and *The Last Battle*, but he

---

[6] I have always found it curious that my favorite Chronicles of Narnia—*The Voyage of the Dawn Treader*, *The Silver Chair*, and *The Horse and His Boy*—are the ones with the fewest scenes set in Narnia proper. I believe only *The Silver Chair* has any Narnia-set scenes at all. But it's not placement that makes something Narnian, as Edmund points out in the first

might as well have "just friends" stamped on his forehead. Jill Pole would back me up here.

4. PRINCE RILIAN

Speaking of *The Silver Chair*, its long-term occupant spends the majority of his page time as a pompous git who reminds Jill of Hamlet and laughs way too much. By the time the enchantment is broken, we're already a bit turned off, not to mention wary that a guy who has been under a spell that long may have some serious baggage to deal with. Who wants to be the chick he dates after that fiasco? "My last girlfriend was stunning. Positively divine in every way. The Lady of the Green Kirtle. How enchanting! Too enchanting, if I can be honest. She had me under an evil spell for a decade, and then she turned into this wretched giant snake and I had to kill her. So . . . what are you doing this weekend?"

I think I'll be washing my hair.

5. SHASTA

A.k.a. Crown Prince Cor of Archenland. Now there's a title to rival the Count of the Western March, and Shasta is a character who's almost as interesting as Edmund. His growth arc over the course of the novel is a joy to behold, and his happy ending as a prince never fails to make me cheer. But who wants to fight Aravis for him? Remember her giant sword? Mazel tov to you both!

------

chapter of *The Voyage of the Dawn Treader*. It's a certain quality of spirit, which is why those in our world can be drawn to Narnia in the first place. They simply *are* Narnian, through and through.

6. DIGORY KIRKE

For me, Digory just came too late in the series for any serious attachment to form. But nowadays, kids are reading *The
Magician's Nephew* first. I wonder how many ten-year-olds start
crushing on the kid (after all, he's got his whole tale of woe,
with the sick mother and the abusive uncle and all) before getting hit with the fact that their favorite is immediately shuffled
off to the role of the old and crotchety professor who doesn't
even seem to have *heard* of Narnia when the Pevensies bring it
up, let alone lets on that he was present during its creation.[7]
The crusty old absent-minded Professor? No thank you.

7. KING TIRIAN

The Last King of Narnia. Is it me, or is Tirian just Caspian
Redux? The only thing I can think of to differentiate the two is
that Caspian had a Mouse for a friend, while King Tirian's best
buddy is the Unicorn, Jewel. Jewel is ten kinds of awesome, but
Tirian? Eh.

Clearly, Edmund is the most eligible of all the Narnian bach-
elors. Plus, given his strong desire to guide other imperfect folks
like Shasta and Eustace down the path of Aslan, he would have
a vested interest in helping me out, were I ever to stumble my
way into Narnia. (And yes, I think I imagined that scenario quite
a bit. Come on, you always checked out the back of wardrobes,
too!)

Of course, at ten I hadn't read a lot of other books, so my
pickings of fictional men were slim. It was pretty much the Nar-

---

[7] Needless to say, this is another reason the books should be read in the
original order.

nians or that dude who had the terrible, horrible, no good, very bad day. As my reading tastes matured, so did my acquaintance with a whole host of heroes *ripe* for literary crushes. However, my early experience with Narnians forever changed my taste in imaginary men. I'd been strongly influenced by Lewis's vision of what makes a hero, and the more I read as I got older,[8] the more I realized that, on some level, I was always looking for another Edmund.

Edmund Paves the Way for Future Literary Crushes

Now, one might suspect that a fan of Edmund would be drawn to the bad boys of literature. Not so. I think those people were fans of angsty, bewitched, Hamlet-esque Rilian. If I liked a bit of badness in my boy, it was only what was left *after* the reformation. I was never into the "tortured" type. No Heathcliffs for me!

I didn't like them perfect, either, but if they sat around all day lecturing girls on how they were bad news, I tended to agree with them, and kept my distance. After all, the Narnians were always a forthright lot. Edmund and his ilk told it like it was. And Edmund, however questionable his past, seemed to have pulled it together. He may have been somewhat graver than Peter, but he was still a cheerful guy, overall. Contrast that with the behavior of the aforementioned Heathcliff, or, in modern times, with the much-beloved Edward Cullen of *Twilight*. (I spent a good deal of that series thinking, "Bella, look at that nice werewolf over there. He seems so much more capable of dealing with his inner darkness, don't you think?") Heck, I might be the

---

[8] Over the next decade, re-reading the series became a yearly event.

only *Buffy the Vampire Slayer* fan I know who liked Riley better than Angel or Spike!

My next big literary crush was Gilbert Blythe who, like Shasta, comes part and parcel with a love interest who was also the heroine of the piece: Anne of *Anne of Green Gables*. Gilbert, like Edmund, spends a good bit of time atoning for his earlier mistakes, though Gilbert's crime was no more serious than a schoolhouse prank (he tugs on Anne's braids and calls her "Carrots," a nickname she abhors as much as her red hair). At the time, I thought Gilbert's teasing of Anne was worthy of her intense and lingering punishment, but now, with age, I wonder why it took her so long to get over it.[9] Didn't anyone ever teach her that the boys who tease you like you? It was the only way I could actually tell when I was in school! Nevertheless, Gilbert reminded me of Edmund, in both appearance and demeanor; he's graver and more sensible than the fanciful Anne, and his wisdom and quietness only mature as he grows older. And, like Edmund, Gilbert is a listener.

I got another twinge of Edmund when I read *Pride and Prejudice* for the first time. While my high school classmates were still swooning over Heathcliff (a crush that I do not, to this day, understand), I was into Mr. Darcy. Like Edmund, he doesn't leave you (or the heroine, Elizabeth Bennet) with the best first impression. He's cranky, rude, unfeeling, and proud. But also like Edmund, he learns that this is not acceptable behavior and makes amends. Yet Darcy is still a reserved man, "graver and quieter" than some of the other men who pop up in the novel. (I later realized that all of Austen's heroes were Edmunds.)

---

[9] By contrast, every time I re-read *The Lion, the Witch and the Wardrobe*, I am confronted anew with how awful Edmund was in that novel.

Still later, when I read Lord of the Rings, shades of Edmund cropped up in the character of Faramir.[10] In Tolkien's books, it was Faramir's brother Boromir who represented the fallen and the treacherous, yet Faramir's personality is much more in keeping with that of King Edmund the Just. He is a scholar who thinks things through before acting, despite the fact that his preferred M.O. (implicit in his close relationship to Gandalf, the "court advisor") earns him the contempt of his father. Faramir is a tad insecure of his place beside his warrior brother,[11] and though he is not known for his abilities on the battlefield, when he needs to fight, he will do so both valiantly and with aplomb. When his father forces him to lead the suicide mission into an Orc-controlled city, Faramir rides off, even knowing it spells certain doom.

He's also acutely aware of and empathetic to the plight of other characters in the story. He recognizes the enormous, impossible task that Frodo has been given (getting that ring to Mount Doom), and in the hobbit, sees a kindred spirit. Neither of them have the ability to do what is being asked of them, but they are more than willing to die trying. Later in the book, in the depressed and sidelined Eowyn, he sees another soul who has experienced disappointment and failure, and he will not let it ruin either of them. (Never was I so happy as when Eowyn saw in Faramir what no one seemed to in Edmund. I vividly remember telling my then-boyfriend that Eowyn *had* to survive her injuries, if only so she could "end up with" Faramir.)

---

[10] I admit that this last one is a bit of a cheat. After all, Tolkien and Lewis were friends, colleagues, and writing companions. Little wonder that their work would contain echoes of the other's.

[11] Boromir, like another of Edmund's siblings, is in possession of a magical horn that can call for help when needed.

I could go on and on, but in the end, it all comes back to Edmund. I know my literary "type": the complex guy who has his feet on the ground, a little experience with pain, a head on his shoulders, compassion for others, and a deep sense of loyalty. He isn't flighty, but nor is he tortured. He's always a shoulder to lean on in times of trouble, and though he's not perfect, he's forgiving of others who are dealing with their own flaws. He likes to solve problems with his brains before he resorts to his muscles, but when fighting is needed, he can hold his own with the best of them. As a novelist, I now write these men.

In real life, I just married one.

✦•✥•❦•❆•✦

Diana Peterfreund is the author of the Secret Society Girl series, as well as *Rampant* and *Ascendant*, two young adult fantasies about killer unicorns. She was raised in Florida and graduated from Yale University in 2001 with degrees in Geology and Literature. A former food critic and an avid traveler, she now resides in Washington, D.C., with her husband and their dog. Like Edmund, she was scared by the White Witch at a young age and still can't stand wintertime. Her website is www.dianapeterfreund.com.

Where will you find St. Brendan in Narnia? And isn't that King Midas hiding over there? In one of the funniest essays you'll find in this anthology, Ned Vizzini presents Lewis by logline to bring you the most entertaining analysis of The Voyage of the Dawn Treader *you're likely to read this year.*

◆•▸▸▓◂◂•◆

Reading the Right Books
The Voyage of the Dawn Treader

NED VIZZINI

The *Voyage of the Dawn Treader* was always my favorite Narnia book, and the wonder of being a kid is that you don't have to question why things are your favorites. That's for psychoanalysis later on. If you had come along and asked me why *Dawn Treader* beat out *The Silver Chair*, which has some really creepy parts, and *The Lion, the Witch and the Wardrobe* (which I always got annoyed by because, in terms of the chronological events of the book, it should have been called *The Wardrobe, the Witch and the Lion*), I would have said that it was because it had cool monsters and lots of amazing islands and various killer enchantments that were really awesome.

But when you grow up you start to understand why you liked these things, and it can be quite sobering. In some cases the only explanation is that you were retarded (see *Duck Tales*, *Barney and Friends*); sometimes you realize with dark horror that the thing played a part in your sexual development (for me, *Ghost Busters*). Sometimes, though, like with *Dawn Treader*, you have a clear and vindicating insight that lets you enjoy the tale as two readers at once—the kid who's wrapped up in it and the adult who sees why they got so wrapped up in it in the first place—and it's this sort of rediscovery and enthusiasm that I heard in my parents' and grandmother's voices when they read Narnia to me.

(I should say my mother's and grandmother's voices. My father read to me too, but it was a different kind of reading; he found this great strategy for putting us all to sleep by reading from *The History of the Persian Empire*, which was, as far as I could tell, the real *Neverending Story*. As soon as my dad started in on the land holdings of Xerxes I was knocked right out.

Later I named my pet lizard Xerxes.)

I mention this to—well, *The History of the Persian Empire* I mention mainly as a suggestion to parents whose kids won't fall asleep—but the rest of it I mention to bring forth the adult insight as to why I liked *The Voyage of the Dawn Treader* so much: it's got a great logline.

A logline is a Hollywood beast: a one-sentence description of a movie that draws you in. For example, *Jurassic Park*: "It's about dinosaurs coming back to life and eating people." *Being John Malkovich*: "It's about people who find a tunnel that goes into John Malkovich's brain." *Jurassic Park 2*: "It's like *Jurassic Park*, with different dinosaurs."

What sets a logline apart from a simple one-sentence description of a work is the intended purpose of making you need to know more. The one-sentence government-sanctioned summary of *Dawn Treader* at the start of my edition reads, "Lucy and Edmund, accompanied by their peevish cousin Eustace, sail to the land of Narnia. . . ." Blah blah blah. That's not the logline. The logline is:

It's About a Bunch of People Who Get In a Boat and Try to Sail to the End of the World

The brave journey into the unknown is the basis of much of children's literature, from *Huckleberry Finn* to *The Phantom Tollbooth*. Neither of those books, however, would elicit much interest or even be recognized by the most important character in *Dawn Treader*: Eustace Clarence Scrubb.

Eustace, one of C. S. Lewis's most satisfying creations, is the consummate boy skeptic. He's so annoying and dour that he "almost deserved" his name, we're told at the start of the book, and in addition to taking special pleasure in the misery of his cousins, Eustace (one of many characters who put Lewis in the continuum of great character-name generators, from Charles Dickens to J. K. Rowling) collects dead beetles and reads "books of information [with] pictures of grain elevators."

Naturally, when he travels to Narnia, Eustace isn't very well-prepared for the adventures that await him. These are loglines that he hasn't seen—especially Reepicheep, the Talking Mouse. (Here I always felt that Lewis overplayed it with the names: we're really supposed to accept a Talking Mouse named Reepicheep? And at the end of the tale, when he bravely relinquishes his leadership, he does it to a guy named Peepicheek?)

Eustace's sudden lack of salient knowledge is an irony that Lewis takes great pleasure in. In the midst of the adventure that transforms him about halfway through *Dawn Treader*, Lewis reminds us three times that Eustace had "read none of the right books" (perhaps he'd been reading *The History of the Persian Empire*), and therefore has no idea what a dragon's treasure hoard is supposed to look like or even—a stretch, but telling—a dragon itself.

Thus, as the *Dawn Treader* travels through the unknown seas east of the Lone Islands, she isn't sailing so much into foreign lands as into foreign stories—places where a knowledge of the everyday is irrelevant, or even encumbering, and the more involved you are with fantasy, folklore, and children's tales, the more likely you are to survive.

Logline: It's About That "Other" Story

If *Dawn Treader* is a story of stories, we have to first address that big one: Christ. C. S. Lewis's importance as a twentieth-century Christian thinker continues to grow as critical support for his scholarship (notably his introduction to *Paradise Lost*) and his arguments for Jesus's divinity outstrip for many what he accomplished with Narnia. It's taken as a given, then, that the Narnia books are Christian allegories.

Lewis hated this. He held that the Narnia series wasn't an allegory at all: instead of *representing* Jesus, Lewis viewed Aslan as a supposition of the form Christ might take if he were sent to redeem citizens of a fantasy realm. He explains in a letter from May 29, 1954, to a group of fifth graders (collected in *Letters to Children*):

> You are mistaken when you think that everything
> in the books "represents" something in this world.
> . . . I did not say to myself "Let us represent Jesus
> as He really is in our world by a Lion in Narnia":
> I said "Let us suppose that there were a land like
> Narnia and that the Son of God, as He became a
> Man in our world, became a Lion there, and then
> imagine what would have happened." If you think
> about it, you will see that it is quite a different
> thing.

It is arguable that the supposition of an event into a fantasy setting is exactly the same as an allegory, so long as the results turn out the same. (For example, let us *suppose* that a group of pigs had to respond to a power vacuum in their farm by enacting Communism.) But in any case, if the Narnia books were just Christian allegories, they wouldn't have sold 100 million copies and influenced all the children's fantasy that has come since. What makes them great are the parts that *aren't* Christian.

Aslan is a drag, really. He's always showing up to tell people what not to do and get them out of tough situations that they really should have been able to get through themselves. (Or he's dying, which is very grave.) The best parts of Narnia, and especially *The Voyage of the Dawn Treader*, are the non-Christian tales that Lewis grabbed from Roman and Greek folklore and, predominantly, from the lore of the European explorers of the North Atlantic. It is their stories, mostly, that Lewis took and strung out across a group of islands stretching east of Narnia.

Logline: It's About a Mouse Who Wants to Find God

Why east? Why *not* east is what the explorers and mythmakers of Medieval and Renaissance Europe wanted to know. They began charting the North Atlantic as early as the sixth century A.D., and while much was made of the gold-seekers, it was the missionaries who both began earliest (the sixth-century explorers were Irish monks) and had the most success establishing and maintaining colonies.

But the monks wondered why the ocean stretched west when clearly, according to Genesis, paradise lay to the east. East was sort of problematic in Europe: that was where the Goths, Persians, Huns, and all sorts of nasty terrain were. So was there a directional mistake somewhere? Did God forget a road sign?

Perhaps you had to go west first and *then* to turn around and go east. This is what the monks ascribed to St. Brendan, the real-life explorer whose travels they turned into legend: he had to sail west for seven years before he could turn east to the Promised Land. Brendan's adventures figure in large part in *Dawn Treader* and give C. S. Lewis a perfect supposition: suppose the Atlantic were to the east of Europe, and the explorers weren't going for land or even to convert people but to find the Kingdom of Heaven.

In the book, Edmund, Lucy, Eustace, and King Caspian X aren't going explicitly to find paradise. They are going to find and return to Narnia seven noble lords that were exiled by Caspian's evil Uncle Miraz. But the lords' names are Lord Revilian, Lord Bern, Lord Argoz, Lord Mavramorn, Lord Octesian, Lord Restimar, and Lord Rhoop—in other words, an absolute mishmash of nonsense that shows off Lewis's nomenclature abilities (Lord Restimar?) more than it adds to the story. The lords' true purpose is to get the plot on its way and add some side tales; none of the lords turn out to be all that interesting, and Caspian can't even remember the name of the unfortunate Lord Rhoop.

> REEPICHEEP: Why should we not come to the eastern
> end of the world? And what might we find there?
> I expect to find Aslan's own country.

This is not a journey to find gold or convert unbelievers or establish civilization. As much as Lewis argues that his stories are not allegories, this is a tale of a spiritual journey to God's Kingdom. Lewis says so himself, in a Narnia series outline in one of his letters, March 5, 1961: "The Voyage of the 'Dawn Treader' the spiritual life (especially in Reepicheep)."

Logline: It's About Life, Death, and Resurrection

To reach the Promised Land, naturally, the first thing one must do is believe. That isn't going to be easy for Eustace, whose skepticism and bad behavior aren't lessened in the slightest by his first month in Narnia. But then, when Eustace leaves the group and ends up in a dragon's lair, he gets involved in one of Lewis's more obvious non-allegory allegories: "Sleeping on a dragon's hoard with greedy, dragonish thoughts in his heart, he had become a dragon himself." In this moment Eustace becomes more than a bratty boy. He becomes a sinner—he takes on the shape of Satan—and immediately wants to repent and return to the people who he now realizes are his friends.

Lewis thus has us set up for a conversion story not dissimilar to his own at the age of thirty. Eustace, as a dragon, is visited by Aslan, who comes to him in a dream and tells him to take off his skin and be born again. Eustace tries, but it doesn't work until Aslan himself rips the skin, digging deep into him with more pain than he has ever known. Then he is transformed back into a boy. Here Lewis makes two points: salvation cannot be attained by works alone (otherwise, Eustace could have pulled off the skin just fine), and the pain of submitting to God is the most difficult pain of all. Lewis said of his own conversion in *Surprised by Joy*: "In the Trinity Term of 1929 I gave in . . . the most dejected and reluctant convert in all England."

Logline: It's About a Guy Who Everything He Touches Turns to Gold

Strange that Lewis would identify *The Voyage of the Dawn Treader* as the story of Reepicheep's spiritual journey when it is Eustace, certainly, who is most changed as the ship begins encountering more islands. He immediately becomes useful to his travel mates as an Aslan-ian, helping fend off a sea serpent (no slouch with his Milton, C. S. Lewis takes advantage of *Paradise Lost*'s equation of Satan's size with that of Leviathan). He then comes to the island of Deathwater, which has a pool that turns everything that touches it into gold.

Lewis mentions *The Odyssey* in a brief preliminary outline for *Dawn Treader*, but aside from the fact that both take place on a ship there isn't a whole lot of correlation. Odysseus, a grizzled man, is trying to get home; Caspian, a bright youth, has just left it. Battle with singular personalities like Polyphemous (or, for that matter, the White Witch) takes a back seat to smaller struggles against natural phenomena and difficult puzzles. Indeed, with all the chances for Dryads and Fauns to appear, Lewis stays clear of them in this book in favor of the Northern European myths, the result being very few Greek references. But we do get a nice retelling of the Midas tale on the island of Deathwater.

King Midas was not a manslaughter case. It wasn't as if he stumbled upon the idea of touching things and turning them into gold. He used to spend all his time thinking about it— about how he would redecorate his place if only he could do just that—a little gold here, a little gold there, gold *feng shui*. When he met Dionysus and was told by the god that he could have one wish, he didn't waste a breath. Dionysus laughed at him before granting it.

C. S. Lewis inverts the Midas story, creating a clear but deadly pool that turns *you* into gold. Midas begs to have his "power" taken away from him only a few days after receiving it, for the simple reason that he can't eat and drink—everything that touches his lips turns to gold. Lewis serves up this nasty image in reverse: were a person to crouch and drink from the pool, they would tip over and fall in, quite heavy and dead.

An island of retribution for those who covet gold is only fair in a book about exploration. It's satisfying to see the stuff get some retribution for all the people who died in search of it, and in this regard C. S. Lewis had other precedents. In *The Travels of Marco Polo*, we hear of a king who loved his treasure so much that Genghis Kahn trapped him in his tower with it, telling him, "If you love it so much, eat it!"

(A similar scene takes place at the end of the 1999 Brendan Frasier film *The Mummy*. Just as important.)

Logline: It's About These Invisible Guys with One Foot and How They Get Visible Again

C. S. Lewis never neglected humor in his novels, usually in the form of casual, dry English asides (often in parentheses, directly addressed to the reader, like this, except funny), but he hits a high note in *Dawn Treader* on the island of the initially invisible one-footed Dufflepuds. Their inability to get anything done due to constant yes-manning and babbling makes them hugely entertaining, but when they first appear as disembodied voices, they are quite scary indeed, and they're not without precedent.

In the sixteenth century it was widely known among European seafarers that an island called the Isle of Demons lay north of Newfoundland, from which could be heard (according to a book called *Phantom Islands of the Atlantic*, by Donald Johnson), "a great clamor of men's voices, confused and inarticulate." As it turned out, the island was home to immense quantities of sea birds: gannets, great awks, murres, and frigates. The inhuman noise they created would make anyone think it held demons. (The smell of the guano wasn't great, either, and nowadays the island is called Funk Island.)

Lewis understood the irony here—a bunch of men afraid of a bunch of birds—and took it for his story. When he reveals the Dufflepuds, he reveals them to be monopods, absurd and innocuous one-footed men, who are likewise taken from a legend. Monopods were described as far back as Pliny the Elder, who portrayed them in *Natural History* almost exactly as Lewis does:

> [They] have only one leg, but are able to leap with surprising agility . . . [T]hey are in the habit of lying

on their backs during extreme heat and protecting themselves from the sun by the shade of their feet.

The mythical monopod was likely taken from secondhand stories of Indian yogis who spent hours standing on foot. Peaceful in life, peaceful in legend.

Logline: It's About a Table of Everlasting Food That You're (Not?) Supposed to Eat

The myth of St. Brendan, the monk who had to sail west to come east, is most referenced toward the end of *Dawn Treader*. Fifty-five days into his journey, the saint encountered a rocky island with an abandoned town and an empty great hall; when he went inside, lo and behold, the table was filled with a feast for him and his men! Now, we all know what's going to happen here, right? Brendan *ordered* his men not to take anything from the room, but apparently no one saw *Indiana Jones*, and somebody got killed.

Similarly, when Eustace and the others reach an island with a table full of food, Caspian orders that nobody even *think* of going near it. And then Lewis pulls up another vivid image from the explorers of the North Atlantic: birds. Thousands of them, blinding white, come to the table and pick it dry.

Birds feature heavily in the St. Brendan myth. After a year of traveling, Brendan encounters enough of them on a tree to completely cover its leaves and branches, making it ash-white. One of them flies to him and advises that he will need to travel for six more years before reaching Paradise. Thus birds act as angels, a nice marriage of Christian and Irish beliefs; in Celtic myth it is birds who serve as supernatural receptacles of worthy human souls.

But Lewis does one nifty twist on the birds and the tables. (Turns the tables on the tables? No. Sorry.) When these birds come and pick the table clean, the food comes right back the next day, so it's entirely acceptable for Caspian's crew to eat it. Like Christ, it is constantly renewed.

Logline: It's About What Happens When You Die

The end of *The Voyage of the Dawn Treader* is a bit woozy. Lit up by an increasingly bright sun, the characters stop sleeping or even talking very much. It was generally believed by all European explorers that the further east one traveled, the brighter the sun would become, but there is another parallel here: the journey into the extreme east is a journey into death. People who have near-death experiences don't say that they saw "a great darkness." It's always a light that is sucking them in.

The final chapters see Lucy encountering a race of sea people who, due to the extreme clarity of the ocean, appear to be just beneath the surface of the water. This too has precedent in the secondhand stories and myths of the exploration of the North Atlantic. Many places that were thought to be "islands" were in fact ridges or sandbars very close to the surface, and ships sailing over them would assume that they were islands that had recently sunk, complete with their own civilizations. St. Brendan encounters a visible sea floor on his long journey, and it is important to remember that behind his mythical voyage was a real voyage that had real visible sea floors. In 1976 Irish explorer Tim Severin reconstructed St. Brendan's purported journey to Newfoundland and found, along the way, just such island ridges, as well as the birds, walruses, leaping porpoises, and icebergs that informed much of the St. Brendan myth—and Narnia.

Logline: It's About All Having Universal Peace Forever

When they finally reach the end of the world, the explorers in *Dawn Treader* encounter a great wave that stays in place. One of the mythical islands of the North Atlantic, Hy-Brazil, was called "The Land Under the Wave"; its placid nature suggests the complete majesty over the earth that Aslan exhibits in his realm. In order to return home, Eustace and his cousins encounter Aslan (in the form of a lamb) and cross a river to get back to England. Here one might be tempted to think about the river Styx. But Lewis has other ideas in mind. From Revelations:

> Then the angel showed me the river of life-giving water. . . . On either side of the river grew the tree of life.

A river was said to bisect the legendary island of Hy-Brazil, which European explorers at the time recognized as St. Brendan's "Paradise." With paradise on both sides, Eustace and Lucy are going to be fine whether in our world or in Narnia.

The Voyage of the Dawn Treader shows us that there's a lot of good in useless fantasy books, in case you actually do end up in a magical world. If you know about Midas, about St. Brendan, about not getting fooled by strange voices, and about always, *always* not touching things, you should do very well. If you don't, you're going to be screwed. Everybody understands this, even Aslan, who asks Lucy, when she accidentally makes him invisible, "Do you think I wouldn't obey my own rules?"

And Eustace, far from just being a good Christian, is by the end of the book a mythology expert. When Reepicheep suggests tying King Caspian to the mast, he says, "Like they did with Ulysses when he wanted to go near the Sirens."

That's reading the right books.

Ned Vizzini is the author of three acclaimed young adult books: *It's Kind of a Funny Story* (now a major motion picture from Focus Features), *Be More Chill*, and *Teen Angst? Naaah . . .* Ned speaks to students and teachers at schools, universities, and libraries about writing and mental health. He also reviews books for *The New York Times* and *L Magazine*. He lives in Brooklyn and Los Angeles. His work has been translated into seven languages.

Of course you know the spiritual messages of Narnia. Of course you realize the Great Lion Aslan is a metaphor for Christ. But suppose you missed all that the first time you read the books . . . and maybe even the second? Well, join the club. Sarah Beth Durst is here to say you're not the only one—and more to the point, it doesn't matter.

◆•▶●◆●◀•◆

Missing the Point

SARAH BETH DURST

Remember *Bambi*? Cute deer. Cute bunny. Cute skunk. Very scary forest fire. Very traumatic death of Bambi's mother. . . . Yeah, I don't actually remember that last part. Seriously, when I saw *Bambi*, I didn't realize that his mother died. I thought that Bambi's parents were simply divorced and now it was time for his dad to have custody. Later, I was the kid in high school English who argued that Robert Frost's "Stopping by Woods on a Snowy Evening" wasn't about suicide. I thought it was a very nice poem about a pretty New England forest like the one behind my house, which was quite lovely, dark, and deep. So as you might imagine, I was also the kid who totally missed all the religious symbolism in the Narnia books.

But I still loved the books.

Why? Why do these books hold such sway over the hearts and imagination of the thousands of people like me who simply didn't notice the pervasive and often overt Christian references that are at the heart of the novels? Why are they still meaningful to people who completely missed the point?

The Cat's Meow

Let me first say that the religious references are absolutely there. No question. If you don't believe me, just Google C. S. Lewis. Go on. I'll wait.

See? Very religious man.

Just like I'm 99.9 percent sure that Disney meant for Bambi's mother to (euphemistically speaking) meet God, I'm also 99.9 percent sure that C. S. Lewis meant for the Lion Aslan to (allegorically speaking) *be* God.

But does the reader need to realize that to appreciate the books?

C. S. Lewis ensures that Aslan is a powerful presence in all seven Narnia books. He's often the story catalyst and/or the story conclusion. In *The Lion, the Witch and the Wardrobe* he sacrifices himself to save Edmund (thus ensuring that the prophecy of the four thrones in Cair Paravel can be fulfilled), he breaks the spell on the stone victims of the Witch (thus ensuring that Peter's army has the necessary reinforcements), and he kills the Witch (thus ensuring that the Witch is, um, killed). In *The Horse and His Boy*, he appears as various lions (and once as a cat) to help Shasta and Aravis on their journey. He drives them together, metes out punishment, and then protects them from harm. In *The Silver Chair*, he instructs Jill Pole on how to find the lost prince. In *The Last Battle*, he banishes the demon Tash and then calls for the end of the world.

But it's not just what Aslan does that makes him a strong figure. He has a presence even when he isn't present. When Mr. Beaver mentions Aslan for the first time in *The Lion, the Witch and the Wardrobe*, the Pevensies all have an immediate visceral reaction. "At the name of Aslan each one of the children felt something jump in its inside. Edmund felt a sensation of mysterious horror. Peter felt suddenly brave and adventurous. Susan felt as if some delicious smell or some delightful strain of music had just floated by her. And Lucy got the feeling you have when you wake up in the morning and realize that it is the beginning of the holidays or the beginning of summer." C. S. Lewis conveys Aslan's power and importance in the response of every character to him. Even if you have never heard the phrase "king of kings" before, you understand what it means here. You understand what it means for Aslan to be a Lion-with-a-capital-L. You can see Aslan's awesomeness in both senses of the word purely through the context of the stories. Lewis gives you enough clues that you can be clueless and still get his meaning—you can grasp his concept of God (Lion-with-a-capital-L) without ever realizing he's actually talking about God.

Decorating Your Evil Lair

But what about characters who aren't exact parallels to their theological counterparts? How does the clueless reader understand them?

For example, there's no obvious Satan in the book. We don't have a fallen angel or cloven-footed red guy. There's no fire or brimstone. Instead we have snow and ice. We have Jadis, the White Witch, the last Queen of Charn.

If Aslan is God, then it's not a big leap to say that the White Witch is Satan. But since the first allegory went *whoosh* over my head and since I wasn't very good at leaping anyway (seriously, some kids are late walkers, but I was a late jumper—as a toddler, I'd toss my arms in the air, stick out my belly, and shout "jump," and my feet wouldn't leave the floor), I missed any Satan/Lucifer/devil references with the White Witch. I did, though, find her a highly effective villain, even without any awareness of the allegory. In other words, I didn't need to know that she was a stand-in for Satan in order to appreciate the depths of her villainy.

The Magician's Nephew tells the backstory of the White Witch. Two humans, Digory (who later becomes the Professor in *The Lion, the Witch and the Wardrobe*) and his neighbor Polly, find her in an enchanted sleep on a lifeless planet. Digory wakes her, and the Witch recounts how she single-handedly decimated her world, deliberately destroying every single life form on it (except for herself), because she couldn't be queen.

Yeah, she has a few issues.

In *The Lion, the Witch and the Wardrobe*, the White Witch shines as a deliciously evil villain. With her magic wand, she turns her enemies into stone statues. Her castle is chock-full of them. We see them with Edmund as he enters the courtyard: "They all looked so strange standing there perfectly life-like and also perfectly still, in the bright cold moonlight, that it was eerie work crossing the courtyard." Talk about an awesome evil lair. She decorates it with her enemies.

Think too of how chillingly cruel she is in the Stone Table scene. She isn't content to simply kill Aslan. She orders his mane to be shaved off so that her followers can mock him before he dies. She also has a shiver-worthy final line before she strikes the killing blow: "Understand that you have given me Narnia forever, you have lost your own life and you have not saved his. In that knowledge, despair and die." Ouch.

The White Witch doesn't need to be seen as a direct parallel to Satan to be understood as evil. C. S. Lewis is able to establish her as a source of evil through her actions and through others' reactions to her. In fact, he sets her up as the Bad Guy before we even meet her by showing us Faun Tumnus's fear of her.

Dear Faun Tumnus! This nervous, noble, sweet Faun is one of the most memorable characters in the Narnia books. Or at least, he certainly sticks in my mind, filling space that would otherwise be taken up by 1980s song lyrics. (I admit I have a soft spot for Faun Tumnus. We have a lamppost out in front of our house, and I always call it the Faun Tumnus Lamppost.) In the novels, we first see him mincing toward us through the snow on his goat hooves. "He was only a little taller than Lucy herself and he carried over his head an umbrella, white with snow. . . . He had a strange, but pleasant little face, with a short pointed beard and curly hair, and out of the hair there stuck two horns, one on each side of his forehead." When he sees Lucy, he drops all the packages he's carrying and says, "Goodness gracious me!" (A side note: this always cracks me up because I picture Fauns and Satyrs as the rednecks of mythology. They're traditionally known more for drunken debauchery than good manners, but Faun Tumnus is so perfectly prissy.) Because he's such an appealing character (and the first Narnian we meet), he is responsible for determining the readers' allegiance. Tumnus tells us who the good guys are and shapes our view of the White

Witch. As Lucy later summarizes, "She isn't a real queen at all. . . . She's a horrible witch, the White Witch. Everyone—all the wood people—hate her. She has made an enchantment over the whole country so that it is always winter here and never Christmas." If we'd met the White Witch first, we might have been like Edmund and been ensnared by her Turkish Delight. But we get to know dear Faun Tumnus first, and when we see what happens to him because of his kindness to Lucy, we have a personal stake in wanting to see the Witch defeated. We don't need to be rooting for Aslan to defeat the Witch for the sake of any allegory, no matter how deep or deftly drawn; we're already rooting for Aslan for the sake of Tumnus. In other words, we don't need any references outside the story itself to understand and appreciate the dichotomy between Aslan and the Witch. We don't need to see them as God and Satan to understand their roles. It's all already in there.

Not Obi-Wan Kenobi

Let's talk for a minute about the Witch and Aslan's big show-stopping moment. (Suddenly, I'm picturing a big song and dance routine with the Witch, Aslan, and the Beavers performing Rockette kicks. . . . Oh, that is so very wrong.) Of course I mean the moment of Aslan's sacrifice in *The Lion, the Witch and the Wardrobe*.

Aslan allows himself to be killed by the White Witch as payment for Edmund's treachery. Because he is a willing sacrifice, Aslan is then resurrected, thanks to a deeper magic than the Witch knows. This is the scene most often mentioned as an obvious allegory to the Crucifixion and Resurrection of Jesus Christ.

Of course, the first thousand times I read *The Lion, the Witch and the Wardrobe*, I failed to notice any allegory. Wait, that's not true—I did notice a parallel between Aslan's death and Obi-Wan Kenobi's death in *Star Wars*. Obi-Wan warns Darth Vader, "If you strike me down, I shall become more powerful than you could possibly imagine." Same sort of thing happens with Aslan, except he doesn't warn the Witch. But given that C. S. Lewis most likely didn't watch *Star Wars* before writing the Narnia books, I'm betting that George Lucas was not his source material. At any rate, I missed the (very clear and real) Crucifixion references.

But I *didn't* miss the horror of the scene when all the nightmarish creatures mock Aslan as the Witch raises the stone knife. I *didn't* miss the sweet sadness of the mice who gnaw away the ropes after the Witch and her followers leave. And I *didn't* miss the glory of Aslan's return or the joy of the romp through the morning. I know that I cried the first time I read the Stone Table scene, not knowing that Aslan was coming back. I cried for the horrible waste, I cried for Lucy's loss, and I cried for Narnia. It didn't matter that I hadn't noticed the allegory. I was *inside* the story, and it touched me.

I believe that is what a good book should do: sweep you inside the story so that the characters' joys and losses become your joys and losses. Everything else (moral, theme, allegory) is secondary. This is not to say that they are unimportant. Not at all! The Christian references in the Narnia books (and in the Stone Table scene in particular) add depth, richness, and resonance. But I believe that it's the ability of the story to succeed on its own that gives a novel its staying power. I experienced the Stone Table scene as the sacrifice of Aslan, the great Lion-with-a-capital-L that I loved. If I'd been cognizant of the allegory as I read, I would have been too busy drawing parallels to fully experience the scene. I would have been too distant from the story to have cried—and the novel wouldn't have stayed in my heart for as long as it has.

It's the End of the World as We Know It (and I Feel Fine)

As a counterexample, there were two Narnia books that did *not* stay in my heart. (Sorry, C. S. Lewis!) In two of the books, the allegory does overwhelm the story—and as a consequence, the books lack staying power.

The Last Battle is a direct reference to Revelations. Um, I should put in a disclaimer here. If you haven't noticed yet, I'm not exactly a biblical scholar—for a large part of my childhood, I thought Christmas was Santa Claus's birthday—so I'm going to steer clear of details in the interest of not sounding like a total idiot. (As a general rule, I prefer to avoid looking like a complete idiot whenever possible. It's one of my daily goals.) But I think it's safe to say that the final Narnia book is Revelations. I mean, the world ends. "With a thrill of wonder (and there was some terror in it too) they all suddenly realized what was happening. The spreading blackness was not a cloud at all: it was simply emptiness. The black part of the sky was the part in which there were no stars left. All the stars were falling: Aslan had called them home." And then the sun explodes. Unlike with the death of Bambi's mother, there isn't really any way to misconstrue the fact that virtually every single character from all seven books is now dead. For readers as dense as I am, Aslan even says flat-out: "There *was* a real railway accident. Your father and mother and all of you are—as you used to call it in the Shadowlands—dead. The term is over: the holidays have begun. The dream is ended: this is the morning."

This is not handled with any degree of subtlety. Sun exploding = not subtle. So unlike with Bambi's mother, I did not miss the basic plot points. But I did forget it. When I returned to re-read *The Last Battle* for this essay, I discovered I had zero memory of this rather dramatic and lengthy scene. It had failed to take root in my imagination in the same way that the equally biblical Stone Table scene did.

I also had similar problems with *The Voyage of the Dawn Treader*. I did at least remember this book, but it never held the place in my heart that some of the other Narnia books do. I think Lewis got so caught up in the message of this book (the allegorical spiritual journey) that he forgot to ensure that the adventure (the actual physical journey) made sense. In this novel, King Caspian is sailing away from Narnia on a quest for seven men and the edge of the world—Aslan's Country. Why? I understand the need to find the missing men. I even understand the desire to explore to the edge of the world. But why does Caspian go? Wasn't there someone else he could send? I mean, he's got a kingdom to run. Yes, he left a good regent, but he's the king! Look at what happened to England when King Richard went poncing off to the Crusades—things got so bad there that the people needed Robin Hood—a vigilante—to protect them. (And while this led to the fabulous Disney movie with Robin Hood as a fox, it also led to Kevin Costner's film. Why risk that with Narnia?) Why does Caspian want to reach Aslan's Country himself, especially when reaching it means never returning to Narnia? I think this is just plain irresponsible of him. Even

Caspian's own people point out his selfishness. Reepicheep says, "You are the King of Narnia. You break faith with all your subjects, and especially with Trumpkin, if you do not return. You shall not please yourself with adventures as if you were a private person."

Reepicheep, the warrior Mouse, *does* go on and never returns to Narnia, which also doesn't make a whole lot of sense to me. Why is this great hero depriving Narnia of his strength and bravery before he's old? If I'm reading the allegory correctly, Aslan's Country is Heaven. Why is Reepicheep, the bravest creature in all Narnia, committing suicide? And why does the heroic King Caspian want so desperately to join him?

If I were more familiar with the texts and tenets of Christianity, would I appreciate these two books more? Would I understand better why Caspian and Reepicheep want to find Aslan's Country? Would I see the death and destruction in *The Last Battle* as a happy ending? (Did I mention that they all *die*?) Maybe I would, and maybe I have just poked very large holes in my thesis here (oops). But I think that if the reader needs to access outside knowledge to understand a story, then the story loses power. Regardless of what the message is and regardless of its import, the act of thinking about something outside of the story disrupts the flow of the narrative. So by focusing too much on message, Lewis actually *weakens* that message's impact.

Lewis succeeds better in other books, such as *The Horse and His Boy*. In that book, the characters are (quite sensibly) fleeing a horrible fate. The adventure is center stage, and so we journey along with them, absorbing themes and morals in a more effective way: *through* the story rather than *instead of* the story.

Of course the book where Lewis succeeds most brilliantly is *The Lion, the Witch and the Wardrobe*. In it, the characters explore, escape, befriend, betray, fight, and win in accordance with their personalities, rather than to fit a plot contrivance or a particular message. This book is the most famous and beloved novel of the series. It's also the one that focuses the most on the story. Coincidence? Methinks not. Lewis is at his most powerful (and memorable) when he delivers story first and message second.

Sure, It's a Nice Garden, But Does It Have Tomatoes?

The Magician's Nephew is another example of a story with a subtle-as-a-sledgehammer allegory that isn't overwhelmed by its allegory. *The Magician's Nephew* clearly references Genesis. It's a creation story. Aslan sings the world into existence in a very "let there be light" sort of way. There's even a temptation-in-the-garden scene that goes as far as to have the Witch use the word "knowledge" as she tempts Digory with an apple: "If you do not stop and listen to me now, you will miss some knowledge that would have made you happy all your life." It also has its own Adam and Eve in the form of the cabby and his wife. (In case you missed this reference in *The Magician's Nephew*, Lewis describes them in *The Last Battle* in this way: "These two were King Frank and Queen Helen from whom all the most ancient Kings of Narnia and Archenland are descended. And Tirian felt as you would feel if you were brought before Adam and Eve in all their glory." Not exactly subtle.)

But this highly unsubtle novel also has elements that are purely Narnian. For example, it includes the origin of the lamp-post. The Witch throws a metal bar at Aslan as he creates the world of Narnia. When the bar lands, it begins to grow like everything else affected by Aslan's magic. It sprouts into a lamppost. To the best of my knowledge, there's no religious allegory involved here. This scene merely explains why there's only one lamppost and why it isn't near any house or road. It's details like this that allow the novel to transcend the underlying allegory.

Even the temptation scene mentioned above has its own Narnian flair and doesn't require Bible knowledge to understand. The White Witch offers Digory an apple, which she says will cure his dying mother. But Aslan has instructed Digory to bring the apple back to him, so Digory has to make a terrible, gut-wrenching choice. Frankly, I doubt that I'd have the strength to make the same choice, but Digory (unlike me and unlike the biblical Adam) chooses to take the apple to Aslan rather than using it. As a reward, he is given another apple to cure his mother, and the core of that apple grows into the tree that later becomes the magic wardrobe.

Oh, the magic wardrobe! That wonderful, fabulous wardrobe! This is one of the enduring images of Narnia and is undoubtedly responsible for the continued existence of this type of (very large and heavy) furniture. Who doesn't want to step into a wardrobe and through to Narnia? As with the wardrobe and the lamppost, the creation story in *The Magician's Nephew* is specifically a Narnian creation story. Though it was inspired by Genesis, it stands on its own. And it works as its own story because it is internally logical—and because all the Narnian details are cool.

I Want a Talking Horse

All the Narnian details *are* cool. The Talking Beasts, for instance, fulfill a favorite fantasy of thousands of readers. Okay, maybe just mine, but haven't you ever wondered what an animal would say if it could talk? What would your dog say? ("Food, food, FOOD!") Or the gorilla in the zoo? ("I think, therefore I am.") Or the neighbor's cat? ("Psst, my mistress wears purple underpants.") In the Narnia books, C. S. Lewis gives us a whole country of Talking Animals to daydream about—and also to care about. Even though we may never have met a Talking Deer (outside of Bambi), we immediately understand the horror in *The Silver Chair* that the Marsh-wiggle Puddleglum feels when he realizes he's been eating a Talking Stag. He "was sick and faint, and felt as you would feel if you found you had eaten a baby." I think that's the most memorable (and nightmarish) scene in that entire book, and the fact that it succeeds as being so horrifying shows how compelling the fantasy of Talking Animals is.

As far as I know, the Talking Animals don't have anything to do with any religious allegory. Like the lamppost, they are a purely Narnian element. And they are part of what makes these books special.

Personally, I believe that any story can be improved by the addition of a talking animal or two, and I'm not the only writer who thinks this. Thousands of magical creatures walk through hundreds of fantasy books, courtesy of writers who were inspired by the Chronicles of Narnia. Yes, I know there were plenty of talking animals and magical creatures in stories before Lewis's books, but for many of us, Lewis was the one who first brought talking trees and Fauns to life for us and (more importantly) made us care about them.

Seriously, who doesn't want to hang out with Lewis's Talking Animals? After a long, tiring day, it would be so nice to have

Mrs. Beaver clucking over you and fixing you a spot of tea and a hot marmalade roll. And who doesn't want to ride a Talking Horse? I know I desperately wanted a Talking Horse when I was younger. (I didn't want a real horse, of course. I was petrified of riding. To be fair, I was petrified of anything that looked like it could result in a broken neck. You might say "wimp"; I prefer "healthy survival instinct.") Anyway, a Talking Horse is entirely different from a real horse. I thrilled to the escape of Shasta and Aravis on the backs of the Talking Horses Bree and Hwin in *The Horse and His Boy*. I imagined myself galloping across fields and farms on Bree's back while he told me tales of Narnia and the North. . . .

There's a lot to love in these books, and a lot of it (like the Talking Beasts) is utterly independent of religious allegory. In fact, I bet if you ask a hundred kids what they think of when you say the word "Narnia," you won't find one kid who says, "Ooh, those religious themes!" But you will find kids who mention Faun Tumnus, the White Witch on her sledge, the lamppost, the wardrobe, Reepicheep, the Gentle Giants, the Beavers, Aslan. . . . The symbolism and religious message in these books is important and valuable, of course, but grasping it isn't a prerequisite to valuing the books.

The Point

And that's why it's okay that I missed the "point." There's so much else in this series to get. It's a smorgasbord of meaningful moments and memorable characters, thrilling adventures and captivating places. It's okay to miss the point because, regardless of any allegory or any meaning that we as readers impose from the outside, at its heart, the Chronicles of Narnia is a wonderful story. And this is, perhaps, the most important point of all.

As Lewis says in *The Horse and His Boy*, "For in Calormen, story-telling (whether the stories are true or made up) is a thing you're taught, just as English boys and girls are taught essay writing. The difference is that people want to hear the stories, whereas I never heard of anyone who wanted to read the essays." Um . . . well . . . yeah . . . what I mean is . . . oh, crap.

<hr>

Sarah Beth Durst is the author of *Enchanted Ivy* and *Ice* from Simon & Schuster and *Into the Wild* and *Out of the Wild* from Penguin Young Readers, fantasy adventures that include neither wardrobes nor lampposts but are chock-full of magic polar bears, witches, princes, and were-tigers. She began writing fantasy stories at age ten after many failed attempts to find magical kingdoms inside her closet. She holds an English degree from Princeton University and currently lives in Stony Brook, NY, with her husband, her children, and her ill-mannered cat. She also has a pet griffin named Alfred. (Okay, okay, that's not quite true. His name is really Montgomery.) For more about Sarah, visit her online at www.sarahbethdurst.com.

Could it be true? Could the magic be real? Does evil stalk our world in much the same way it stalks the worlds of fiction? Have men and women lived through a real-life war of Light and Darkness? I've delved into some of history's gloomiest corners to show that C. S. Lewis may have themed his work on a magical conflict he actually experienced.

◄ ►►❊►❍◄ ►

The War of Light and Darkness

HERBIE BRENNAN

The Chronicles of Narnia is a seven-book tale of good versus evil—the age-old war of Light and Darkness. It's a story you'll also find in the Lord of the Rings, the Harry Potter series, and many other fantasy novels—a heady brew of myth and magic, brave heroes, dark villains, mystic artifacts, and occult powers.

But that's all just fiction—right? You'd never get black magicians, mystic artifacts, and occult powers in the real world, would you?

Well . . .

The author of the Narnia chronicles, Clive Staples Lewis, fought in the First World War. He joined the British Army in

1917, and was commissioned an officer in the third Battalion of the Somerset Light Infantry. He fought at the Somme and was subsequently wounded during the Battle of Arras.

He was forty years old when the Second World War broke out, a Fellow of Magdalen College, Oxford. Just four years after the war ended, he began writing *The Lion, the Witch and the Wardrobe,* the first of his Narnia Chronicles. Was the book inspired, at least in part, by the war he'd just lived through?

Before we tackle that important question, we need to ask another: could World War II be reasonably described as a War of Light and Darkness?

Conventional historians dismiss the notion. They see it as a conflict arising out of political, social, and economic issues. Your school history books will typically lay emphasis on the Treaty of Versailles (which ended World War I with humiliating terms for Germany), on the doctrine of *lebensraum* (living space) which fuelled Hitler's expansionist policies, on secret Nazi rearmament, on the Allied policy of appeasement that encouraged Nazi ambitions.

But while all these factors were unquestionably relevant, there were deeper, darker forces at play, still largely unsuspected more than sixty years later, yet perhaps sensed by the finely tuned instincts of an author who lived at the time. Let's examine the evidence for those forces now.

In October 1907, an eighteen-year-old Austrian schoolboy applied for admission to the Viennese Academy of Art and was turned down because his test drawings were poor. Instead of returning to his home at Linz, he stayed in Vienna. Even after his money ran out in 1907, he hung on, living like a tramp, for six more years.

The boy was Adolf Hitler. Your history books won't mention it, but during that period he became a black magician.

According to Dr. Walter Johannes Stein, who was confidential adviser to British Prime Minister Winston Churchill during WWII, Hitler developed an interest in Medieval magic and made a profound study of Oriental mysticism, astrology, yoga, and hypnosis. One of the places where he followed these interests (claims the U.K. historian Trevor Ravenscroft) was the secondhand bookshop of a man named Ernst Pretzsche.

Pretzsche was a baddie to match the worst villains of Narnia—a fat, sinister, toad-like hunchback with warts. He had something of a reputation for encouraging students along the troubled road of occult practice. When he saw the sort of books Hitler looked at, he took an interest at once. Before long, Pretzsche had become the young man's teacher of the dark arts.

As a sorcerer's apprentice, Hitler quietly abandoned any leanings he might have had toward mysticism and yoga and turned instead to what's called the Western Esoteric tradition, a body of magical lore passed down the centuries by European wizards. He embarked on a daily routine of graded meditations and visualization exercises based on secret symbolism Pretzsche claimed to have discovered in the Grail Cycle—the ancient body of stories told in Medieval times about King Arthur and his Knights of the Round Table.

The training took years and may well have been the thing that kept Hitler in Vienna long after any sensible young man would have gone home. But the day eventually came when Pretzsche told Hitler he was ready for initiation into the deeper mysteries of magic. And at this point their relationship took a distinctly sinister turn.

Pretzsche's father was a botanical chemist who had spent much of his career in Mexico studying the peyote cactus. Pretzsche himself lived for many years in South America and, upon his father's death, brought back specimens of the cactus to Europe, where it was completely unknown at the time. He still had these specimens when he met up with Hitler.

Peyote is a hallucinogenic plant that, today, is seen as part of the world's "recreational" drug problem. Pretzsche used it for a very different purpose. During a ritual ceremony of initiation, he fed it to Hitler as a religious sacrament. To an unsuspecting youth from a culture that knew nothing whatsoever about psychedelic drugs, the effect must have been devastating, whirling him out of ordinary consciousness into a vision of his destiny that would later plunge the whole world into war.

The experience changed Hitler profoundly. August Kubizek, a young man who occasionally shared rooms with him, remarked, "I was struck by something strange which I had never noticed before . . . it was as if another being spoke out of his body and moved him as much as it did me."

Hitler left Vienna in 1913. When WWI broke out the following year, he enlisted in the First Company of the 16th Bavarian Reserve Infantry Regiment. A fellow volunteer was Rudolf Hess, a young German with occult contacts about whom we'll hear a little later.

Hitler acted as a motorcycle courier throughout most of the war, and was twice wounded and once decorated for bravery. Shortly after the conflict ended he met up with Dietrich Eckart, a central figure in the *Thule-Gesellschaft*, one of Germany's most powerful secret societies.

Thule-Gesellschaft was a society with some very weird practices. Members involved themselves in ritualistic séances—special meetings, the purpose of which is to make contact with the dead—using a Russian peasant woman as a spirit medium. Past members of the Thule Group, returning from beyond the grave, were called up during these nightmarish rituals and delivered messages through the medium. One such spirit was the Comtesse von Westarp, a former secretary of the Group who had been murdered by the Communists. Her ghost announced the coming of a new Messiah, a leader preparing to take charge of the Thule, and, indeed, the whole German nation.

Dietrich Eckart searched diligently for the new Messiah and soon decided he had found him in Adolf Hitler. The willing pupil was swiftly initiated, taught the secret doctrines of humanity's ancient history, and instructed in the techniques of modern sorcery.

With his mystical background, his training at the hands of Pretzsche, his drug-induced contact with spirit worlds, and his steely conviction of his personal destiny, Hitler proved an apt choice. Before long, the Thule Group was searching for a political front that would enable them to seize power over the entire nation. They found it in the German Workers' Party, a tiny right-wing group Hitler had investigated in his post-war work with the German government in 1919.

Toward the end of the First World War, Hitler fell victim to a British gas attack in France. Temporarily blinded and in a state of collapse, he was removed to a hospital where he eventually learned of the German surrender on November 11, 1918.

After his discharge from hospital, he remained in the army for a short time, drawing army rations and wearing an army uniform. He volunteered for guard duty at a prisoner-of-war camp, but by the end of January 1919 the camp was closed. He returned to Munich and drifted into a job as Instruction Officer with the army's Seventh District Command. It was as much a political as military post—he was required to indoctrinate the troops against socialist, pacifist, and democratic ideas.

Part of his job was to investigate some of the small political parties that were mushrooming in Germany at the time, largely with a view toward finding out which of them was Communist inspired. One that caught his attention was the suspiciously named German Workers' Party.

The Party was not, however, Communist or otherwise leftist in its views. If anything, it stood as far right as Hitler himself. It was tiny and poor (at the time of Hitler's investigation, the treasury stood at less than eight marks), but it exercised sufficient fascination for him to join within weeks.

With Thule Group backing, the German Workers' Party grew dramatically. By 1920 it had changed its name to the National Socialist German Workers' Party—or, as it is better known today, the Nazi Party. By 1921, Hitler was its undisputed leader.

In November 1923, as head of a private army of several thousand storm troopers, Hitler attempted to take over the government of Germany by force—his famous but completely unsuccessful *Kapp Putsch*. The fiasco might well have ended National Socialism for good, except that Hitler used his remarkable powers of oratory to turn his subsequent treason trial into a propaganda victory of international proportions. He constantly harped on the idea that only strong leadership by someone like himself could solve Germany's current economic and political problems.

As a result, he received no more than a short jail sentence and won the support of large numbers of his fellow countrymen.

Ominously, the Thule Group's Dietrich Eckart remarked on his deathbed just one month later, "Follow Hitler. He will dance, but it is I who have called the tune. I have initiated him into the secret doctrine, opened his centres of vision and given him the means to communicate with the Powers. Do not mourn for me: I shall have influenced history more than any other German."

Hitler emerged from jail in 1925 to find his National Socialist Party in such a mess that he practically had to rebuild it. From 1926 onward, it showed a small, steady growth, slowed by laws that put severe limits on its activities. Then, toward the end of 1930, an economic storm broke over Germany. Unemployment skyrocketed and social structures began to crumble. The development was to prove good news for Hitler. Frightened people swarmed to his cause. Soon he began to attract a type of mass following he had never achieved before.

On January 30, 1933, following one of the most turbulent political periods of German history, Adolf Hitler became Chancellor of the German State. From doss house to Chancellery . . . It was a rags-to-riches story of epic proportions, and all the more unlikely when one considers its central character—small in height, unimpressive in appearance, narrow-minded, lazy, and ill-educated. It almost seemed—as the Thule Group certainly believed—that some dark force was working through him.

But Hitler's magical education did not end with the Thule Group. Within that organization was an even stranger figure than the alcoholic Eckart: Karl Haushofer.

Haushofer was a professor at the University of Munich and a former teacher of Rudolf Hess, who introduced Hitler to him. Haushofer, who also belonged to an organization called the Vril Society, was an initiate of a Japanese secret society and a man well experienced in practical magical work.

Haushofer was a Bavarian born in 1869. For most of his working life he was an outstanding professional soldier. He received an early appointment to the Staff Corps, worked for the German Federal Intelligence Service in India and Japan, spoke several Oriental languages fluently, mastered Sanskrit, and became something of an authority on Oriental mysticism.

After his appointment to the University of Munich, Haushofer's ideas spread rapidly throughout Germany. It was he who taught the doctrine of *lebensraum*, which held that the German people (as a master race) were entitled to expand their country eastward, and laced it with an overlay of racialism and mysticism.

While his interest in the occult was not particularly well-known during his lifetime, he did build up a reputation as a psychic during WWI. When he was introduced to Hitler in the early 1920s, he may have recognized the dark-eyed young fanatic as a fellow spirit. Certainly Haushofer, like Ekhart, became convinced that, in Hitler, he had found a channel for occult forces. He visited Hitler often during his imprisonment and was still his confidant and teacher after Hitler came to power in 1933. During that time, he initiated Hitler into deeper and darker occult secrets, culminating in the doctrine of the superman, which claimed that pure-blood Germans were far superior to just about anybody else on the planet.

Haushofer's son, Albrecht, was completely different from his father. As a Staff Major in the German Army, he was involved in the failed attempt to assassinate Hitler in July 1944 and sentenced to death because of it. He had no sympathy with the dark forces he believed to be playing around the Führer. Nor had he the slightest illusions about his father's part in the esoteric drama. In his condemned cell he wrote a poem that was found in his pocket after he had been machine-gunned to death by the SS. Three lines of the work sum up the influence of the master magician Haushofer on his Satanic Führer:

> My father broke the seal
> He sensed not the breath of the Evil One
> But set him free to roam the world

Nazi obsession with the occult did not end when the conspirators came to power and found themselves facing the massive problems of running what was then a shattered country. If anything, it flowered, for Hitler and his new Deputy Führer Hess were not the only senior Nazis with an interest in dark arts.

The overweight airman Herman Goering, given the responsibility of building up the Luftwaffe (German Air Force), was a Thule Group member who graduated from mind-expanding drugs to heroin. He had been "cured" once of narcotic addiction in Langbro Asylum, but the appetite remained. Now he felt his magical powers were great enough to allow him to hold the drug in check. But he was to find, in the bitterness of a few short years, that they were not.

The plump, robotic little civil servant Heinrich Himmler translated his own occult dreams into a black-uniformed reality when he established the SS, an elite militia organized on the pattern of the Jesuit Order. This grim, inverted "Society of Jesus" was headed by a thirteen-strong inner sanctum of generals. They met secretly in a castle in Westphalia to perform esoteric rituals designed to attune them to the heroes of Germany's ancient past. Himmler himself was fascinated by these towering figures of history and believed himself guided by them. He performed a solitary séance once a year in the crypt of Quedlinburg Cathedral to contact the spirit of his Saxon namesake, Heinrich the Fowler, and seek advice on matters of state. (Himmler believed himself to be the reincarnation of King Heinrich, though oddly enough failed to see the contradiction involved in calling up his own ghost.)

Esoteric ideas went far beyond the actions of individuals. They quickly came to influence Nazi policy as a whole. This was nowhere more evident than in the notorious "Final Solution to the Jewish Question." To top-level Nazis, Jews were the remnant of those subhuman races which were spoken of in their weird version of occult prehistory. Jews became the target of deliberate and increasing persecution, culminating in an all-out effort to wipe them out completely—an attempt at genocide that cost 6,000,000 lives.

The Nazi Propaganda Minister, Dr. Josef Goebbels, invented reasons for this policy (the Jews were "too rich," "too powerful," or "owed no allegiance to the German nation"), but the real motive was occult. No one bothered to invent reasons for the Nazi attempt to exterminate the Romani nation, but tens of thousands of gypsies also died in accordance with the doctrine that, as subhumans, they were a biological barrier to the course of esoteric evolution.

The Christian churches, visible symbols of the Forces of Light, became a further target for persecution. Freed from all restraint, the maniac Lord of Thule, Alfred Rosenberg (who became the foremost philosopher of Nazism and an influential force in the Nazi Party from 1933 to 1945), attempted to establish a Nazi Anti-Church, with the Bible replaced by Hitler's turgid autobiography *Mein Kampf* and an iron sword beside the altar.

The odious Dr. Theodor Morell, whose membership in the Thule Group supposedly gave him lunatic insights into healing unavailable to lesser mortals, became the Führer's personal doctor, and proceeded to wreck Hitler's health with quack pills and potions and nonsensical injections.

Despite an early wave of persecution of occultists—or at least those occultists who were not involved with Thule or Vril—top Nazis continued to consult astrologers and mediums in the hope of obtaining supernatural guidance in their aspirations.

When Hitler annexed Austria in 1938, one of his first actions was to order the seizure of a mystic artifact—the *Lancea Longini*, or Spear of Destiny. This ancient weapon, purported to be the spear that pierced the side of Christ while he was dying on the cross, formed part of the Hapsburg dynasty's imperial regalia stored in Vienna. Hitler seems to have been convinced the spear had magical powers. (The spear stayed in Germany until the American general George S. Patton—himself a man of esoteric convictions—arranged for its return to Austria in 1945.)

The lunatic dance continued as the world plunged into war. Hitler made tactical decisions based on psychic impressions and intuition. Haushofer successfully urged that military strategy be based on esoteric considerations and harnessed to esoteric goals. A Pendulum Institute was established in Berlin

so that the location of Britain's Atlantic convoys might be determined by dowsers (people with a psychic ability to find water
and minerals) operating divining rods over maps. Rudolf Hess
flew to Scotland to make peace with Britain on the basis of a
vivid dream and astrological advice. (The author Ian Fleming,
creator of James Bond and himself involved in the British Secret
Intelligence Service, suggested that the British magician Aleister
Crowley be hired to interview him.)

Esoteric considerations halted work for months on Hitler's
advanced rocket weapons. A team of top scientists—and some of
the latest defense equipment—was diverted to a Baltic island in an
attempt to find out whether the Earth was really a bubble within
a universe of infinite rock (an occult theory going around Nazi
circles at the time).

Himmler tried to communicate with his beloved Führer by
telepathy. An entire section of the SS was permanently devoted
to time-wasting studies like the occult properties of the bells at
Oxford or the esoteric significance of the top hat at Eton school.
Expeditions were mounted to Tibet, which was believed to be
the magical capital of the planet. The war was conducted under
guidance from the Beyond, with lines of communication established at secret Thule Group meetings by means of a type of
tarot pack and, oddly enough, a short-wave radio. (Members
believed they were talking to the "King of Terror," a superhu-
man being living somewhere in the Himalayas.) Blood sacrifice
became the order of the day, on a scale never before experienced
by suffering humanity.

It was truly a War of Light and Darkness.

And in 1945 it all collapsed, as the occult supermen of Nazi
Germany were finally defeated by soldiers who, by and large,

saw themselves as no more than ordinary men and women with a job to do, but might, from another, more romantic (but equally real) perspective, be described as warriors in the service of the Light.

The Chronicles of Narnia are not, of course, an allegory of WWII. C. S. Lewis would have been well equipped to recognize strange undercurrents in the conflict that raged around him; although by the time WWII broke out Lewis was again a committed Christian, he had temporarily lost his faith in 1911 and taken an interest in mythology and the occult. But even apart from the central theme of Light versus Darkness, there are elements within the whole sorry Nazi story that may have proven inspirational to C. S. Lewis.

The boy Edmund's betrayal of his family to the White Witch in *The Lion, the Witch and the Wardrobe* was precisely what happened again and again in Germany throughout the 1930s. Children who fell under the spell of Nazi authority, just as Edmund fell under the spell of the Witch, were encouraged to report any transgressions of their parents or their siblings. Many of those who did saw family members dragged off to the concentration camps or gas chambers.

The rise of the White Witch herself parallels that of Hitler. Like Hitler, she appeared benign on the surface but quickly proved to be a tyrant who usurped power over her native land. She even placed a ban on Christmas, a move that echoed the ideas of Hitler's closest henchman, Heinrich Himmler, who tried to abolish Christmas, replacing the celebration with an old pagan festival "for the sake of the children."

But the oddest parallel of all is the icy landscape of the White Witch's perpetual winter. Perhaps the strangest of all the occult influences on Adolf Hitler was that of Hans Hörbiger, a German engineer who developed a cosmology based on falling moons and the eternal conflict of Fire and Ice.

Like the Witch, Hitler believed himself to have control over the weather—a lunatic idea that played a major part in his downfall. Historians agree that the turning point of WWII came when a previously victorious Germany invaded Russia. Hitler was strongly advised against the timing of his move. More than a century earlier, Napoleon had attempted a similar invasion and been defeated by the brutal Russian winter. But Hitler was convinced he had formed a magical alliance with the Powers of Ice and did not bother to equip his troops properly for the approaching snows. They died by the thousands and the tide of war turned.

◆▸▨◂▩▸▨◂◆

Herbie Brennan has a well-established career writing for the children's market—from picture books to teenage fiction, from game books to school curriculum non-fiction. He has produced more than 100 books, many of them international bestsellers, including his GrailQuest series and the teen novel *Faerie Wars*, which was a *New York Times* bestseller along with achieving bestseller status in more than twenty overseas editions.

When you finished your first Narnia book with that feeling of profound satisfaction, you may have believed it was due to the author's masterful characters, his intricate story, his soaring imagination, his marvellously descriptive writing. Diane Duane knows differently. It was the food.

◄►►◄►◄●●►◄●●►

Eating in Narnia
Or, Don't Bother Bringing the Sandwiches

DIANE DUANE

One thing a traveler among universes quickly discovers is that, in many of them, the food's terrible.

This is at least partly a situational problem—a matter of perception. Normally, when people from Earth pass through other fictional universes, they're not there for a pleasure cruise. Normally there's a quest involved, so that they usually wind up running away from something (Orcs, unfriendly armies, assassins, eldritch monsters), hiding from something (ditto), or otherwise getting too preoccupied with local events to care much about the catering. While this is entirely understandable, it's still unfortunate. Unless a given universe's creator is kind to you,

you will never have a chance to sit down and appreciate the local cuisine. Among the less kind (or lazier) creators, you're likely to wind up eating nothing but the fantasy version of fast food: waybread. No matter what kind of valuable life lessons you might learn from such a place, the one that's most likely to stick with you after you get back to earth is straightforward: *Don't go back to that world again without a packed lunch.*

It's a relief, then, for those of us who wander among literary universes, to know that when you need a really good lunch, or a dinner that will stand out in your mind, Narnia is the place to be. It's not that there aren't other universes where food is very important. But even among them, Narnia stands out. Narnia is one of the few universes around from which you'd want to bring home a doggie bag.

There are many reasons for this. The simplest one is that the characters there *like* their food. It's an important part of their lives, and they're not embarrassed about it. It's a fair bet that this is because C. S. Lewis wasn't embarrassed about it either. Anybody could tell this just by looking at a picture of the man as he was in the 1940s and 1950s, when he was writing the Narnia books. All these portraits are—to put it kindly—beefy: images that suggest someone who likes a good meal. But we also know that Lewis's attitudes toward food were enthusiastic because he tells us as much in print.

In his essay "On Three Ways of Writing for Children," Lewis describes two ways of writing for children that he considers really bad. One, he says, is trying to figure out what your target market wants, and then setting out purposely to give it to them. He illustrates this point by mentioning someone who thought that, because Lewis realized he couldn't put sex in his books for young readers, he put food in them instead as a substitute. You can just hear Lewis's gentle scorn in the essay as he says, "I myself like eating and drinking. I put in what I liked to read as a child and what I still like reading now that I am in my fifties."

The exact *kind* of liking for food, though, and what it might be based on, is interesting to look at. Lewis's general attitude toward food in the Narnian world seems to be in broad agreement with that of another now-famous writer for younger readers, J. K. Rowling. This may be because, while Rowling was writing her first work and Lewis was writing the whole Narnia series, they shared a problem: there wasn't a lot of food around. The single mother on income support, writing in cafés to keep warm, also had to economize on her own meals to keep her baby fed. So it's not surprising to see the communal dinner tables at Hogwarts groaning under the weight of all the goodies that world's creator craved and couldn't (initially) afford. But Lewis's food problems were not so unique to him, or so personal. They were shared by everyone in Britain during the period when every book of the Chronicles of Narnia was written. Because Great Britain was at war with Germany.

England, Scotland, Wales, and Northern Ireland, as parts of the British "island nation," routinely imported huge amounts of food—particularly things they couldn't grow themselves because of their climate or lack of suitable farmland. In the 1930s and 1940s more than half of Britain's meat, more than three-quarters of its cheese, sugar, and fruit, and at least *ninety* percent of its grain and fat were imported by ship from Europe, North America, and many other parts of the world. So when war broke out, one of the biggest parts of the Axis Powers' plan to conquer Britain was to cut off its food supply—thereby starving the English, Scots, Welsh, and Northern Irish into surrender. Before cheap air freight, almost all food arrived by ship, so the German navy targeted the merchant ships bringing in this food, sinking as many of them as it could. Only ships traveling in convoys protected by armed naval vessels made it through. And not all of those. Submarines stalked the convoys to pick off inadequately protected ships.

In this desperate situation, the British government had no choice but to start severely limiting, or "rationing," the amount of food its citizens could buy at any one time, so that even with the much-reduced imports of wartime, there was enough to go around for everybody . . . if only *just* enough. Every man, woman, and child was sent a ration book with coupons that had to be taken to the butcher's or grocer's when shopping for food. Each coupon represented a week's ration of something—butter, meat, milk, vegetables, canned goods—and had to be turned in when the purchase was made. Once you'd used up that week's coupons, that was all the food of that kind you could get until the next week. And although a week's ration did make sure that each person had the basic amount of protein, carbohydrates, and vitamins necessary to stay minimally healthy, most everybody was hungry most of the time. This rationing started in 1940 and lasted, in one form or another, straight through until 1954.

So maybe it's no surprise that the first sense you get in Narnia about Lewis's attitude toward food is an air of profound nostalgia for the lost paradise of a varied, ample diet, and a willingness to wallow in the nostalgia somewhat. The very first meal any human experiences in Narnia, the high tea which Mr. Tumnus serves Lucy in *The Lion, the Witch and the Wardrobe*, is a perfect evocation of a turn-of-the-century British tea. Nor is this the hotel-based "high tea" concept, with tinkly china and multiple fancy pastries, but the middle-class tea you would properly have in someone's home, a meal rather than a snack, long on protein, carbs, and comfort. For Lucy, briefly escaped from the middle of the war, and for Lewis, who was as hungry as anyone else in Britain and (some of his letters reveal) as bored by the limitations and substitutions of wartime food, this meal would have smacked of Heaven. It would be years yet before any Oxford don or little English girl could sit down to the delights of a meal that featured fresh eggs and real sardines, a meal in which there was butter for the toast, and actual honey, and cakes with sugar on them. Among Lewis's letters are a number of lyrical thank-you notes to friends or fans who sent him "care packages" of meat and other delicacies from the U.S. and elsewhere. So we can hardly blame him for indulging his longings a little in the world he was starting to invent.

Lewis doesn't exactly restrain himself about this, either. A very short time after Lucy is back in Narnia, this time with her brothers and sister in tow, they are all sitting down for a meal with Mr. and Mrs. Beaver, and it becomes plain that though it may have been winter for a hundred years in Narnia, rationing is no problem there. Fresh trout, and whole hams swinging from the rafters, and seemingly unlimited potatoes, and fresh milk, and "a great big lump of deep yellow butter in the middle of the table, from which everyone took as much as he wanted to go with his potatoes—"

Lewis may sing the praises of the fish in the next paragraph, but during rationing one was allowed only two ounces of butter *per week*. Those who know how people kept even the paper that butter was wrapped in to get the last bit of flavor out of it will know where the real action in that dinner is. And then, as if unlimited butter isn't enough, out comes "a great and gloriously sticky marmalade roll"—not just some kind of one-person pastry, but a rolled cake full of marmalade and drizzled with orange icing—and the teapot. After this final sensory onslaught-cum-sugar rush, no one is able to do much except push back from the table and sigh with contentment. And here Lewis and Rowling agree at heart: the cap of the feast for their characters, the thing that makes it all worthwhile, is having had *enough* to eat. The much-abused Harry, who's lived under the stairs for years scraping by on scanty meals of beans-on-toast while his nasty cousin pigs out (literally) on anything he wants, is unquestionably brother under the skin to these four children from an earlier England who each were allowed only a little more than a pound of meat apiece per week. Those of us who have never known servings much smaller than the Quarter Pounder may be excused if at first we have trouble understanding the real significance of what's going on at the Beavers'.

And the Narnian food message just keeps on being pressed home. Even while they're about to flee for their lives from Maugrim and Queen Jadis's Secret Police, Mrs. Beaver casually packs up what in ration-time England would have been a king's ransom in sugar and other comestibles. Father Christmas comes up with not only magical gifts, but tea (the liberal supply of sugar and jug of cream yet again make it plain that We're Not In England Anymore). The little party of animals that Jadis and Edmund come across shortly thereafter are eating plum pudding (and here we see an extra layer of nostalgia added: the then-unimaginable luxury of a *proper* Christmas plum pudding, full of impossible-to-get suet and dried fruit, and afire with unobtainable brandy . . . completely unlike the valiant but sad fake puddings that people cobbled together during the wartime holidays). A restorative feast is prepared for the children after they meet Aslan for the first time, but little is said about this, as other matters quickly move to the fore. It doesn't matter: we now know, as the children do, that we've come to a Good Place. But it was the concreteness of the food (and the company in which it's been eaten) that left them, and us, ready to deal with the abstracts.

As the Narnian series progressed, back in Lewis's world rationing lessened but did not go away entirely. In *Prince Caspian*, Edmund's remark that he wouldn't mind "a good thick slice of bread and margarine this minute" suggests that butter is still a long way from being taken off the ration lists. (And the margarine of Edmund's time was nothing like the I-can't-believe-it's-not-butter spreads we're used to now: it was a hard, white, nasty, greasy business into which you had to mix the coloring yourself.) Due to the fact that the Narnian culture has been driven underground at this point, the normal nature of the Narnian food takes a while to assert itself: it's eaten in haste or under trying circumstances—a few roasted apples here, a snack of cold chicken and wine there. But once again, the unique personalities associated with the food make the difference: gifts of honey from the Bulgy Bears, nuts from Pattertwig the Squirrel, oaten cakes and apples and herbs and wine and cheese with the Centaurs. The shared nature of the food, the hospitality, is what makes it special here. And for Caspian, "to live chiefly on nuts and wild fruit was a strange experience . . . after . . . meals laid out on gold and silver dishes," but the narrative tells us he had never enjoyed himself more. Then, at last, after the battles that lead to the restoration of Caspian as King of Narnia, come the grapes and magically restoring wines of Bacchus, and the dance of plenty that results in "roasted meat that filled the grove with delicious smell, and wheaten cakes and oaten cakes, honey and many-colored sugars and cream as thick as porridge and smooth as still water" and "pyramids and cataracts of fruit." Narnia is finally coming back into its own, and the food is back with it.

The antique quality of much high-end Narnian food is worth noticing, and this seems to suggest a different kind of nostalgia on Lewis's part. But then so well-read a Medievalist could hardly be expected to avoid borrowing for his world the magnificent excesses of the great feasts of the Middle Ages. One such feast—the one set out daily for travelers who make their way to the Island of the Star near the edge of the world—reflects the best Medieval traditions of food for show as well as for eating, and is said to be "such a banquet as had never been seen, not even when Peter the High King kept court at Cair Paravel." It featured "turkeys and geese and peacocks, there were boars' heads and sides of venison, there were pies shaped like ships under full sail or like dragons and elephants, there were ice puddings and bright lobsters and gleaming salmon. . . ."

This particular preference of Lewis's for older styles of food sometimes expresses itself in negative form as a prejudice against more modern types—though there's no question that in some cases the prejudice is warranted. The sandwiches that the ravenous King Tirian devours in *The Last Battle* are described pretty coolly, especially the ones with "some kind of paste" in them, probably one of the pestilent proto-sandwich spreads of Lewis's youth, "for that is a sort of food that nobody eats in Narnia."

With good reason. These cheap attempted patés still exist in the British and Irish market and still taste terrible.

Only once does a Narnian consciously make an effort to cater to the specifically British tastes of his guest (for elsewhere, the Narnian and British palates seem to mesh fairly well). Coriakin, the "fallen" star and magician of the Dufflepuds' island, says to Lucy, "I have tried to give you food more like the food of your own land than perhaps you have had lately." Not that Lucy has been particularly suffering on the shipboard fare available on the *Dawn Treader*. But this lunch of "an omelette, piping hot, cold lamb and green peas, a strawberry ice, lemon-squash to drink with the meal and a cup of chocolate after" was probably a pleasant restorative for a young girl who had just finished unsettling encounters with such items as the Bearded Glass and the magician's scarily effective grimoire.

"Foreign" food also seems to be something of a minor issue in the books, at least as compared to Narnian fare. We get several good looks at Calormene food both in the casual and formal modes in *The Horse and His Boy*, but they're not all that positive, and the formal food, while opulent enough, isn't described with Lewis's usual care. Shasta, the putative fisherman's son who escapes being sold as slave by running away with the Talking Horse Bree, finds in his saddlebags "a meat pasty, only slightly stale, a lump of dried figs and another lump of green cheese"— uncured, this means, not moldy—"and a little flask of wine." Except for the wine, this doesn't sound particularly appetizing, and the later remark that Shasta finds this "by far the nicest [breakfast] he had ever eaten" seems to reflect the concept that most of his other breakfasts involved fish, stale bread, and water. Also, his later meals, independently obtained on the road, once

again seem to mostly involve bread "and some onions and rad-
ishes." Even his companion-to-be Aravis's provisions, acquired
under less duress, are simply vaguely described as "rather nice
things to eat," and her later meal with the dingbat Tarkheena
Lasaraleen is passed over as "chiefly of the whipped cream and
jelly and fruit and ice sort." (One could make a case that, if Las
seems a little ADD, the Tarkheena's sugar-loaded diet might
have a lot to do with it.) And their last meal together is merely
described as "supper." It's pretty rare for Lewis to be so terse in
a food description.

Then somewhat later, while Shasta's being held by the
royal Narnians who think he's Prince Corin, he is given a meal
"after the Calormene fashion. I don't know whether you would
have liked it or not," Lewis says, going on to describe a very
acceptable hot-weather lunch of whole lobster and chicken-
liver pilaf (though admittedly the snipe stuffed with almonds
and truffles might give some people pause) with any number
of ices and some cold white wine. But the writer's enthusiasm
seems a little muted. One also has to consider in this context
the less-than-positive references to the garlic-and-onion smells
of the marketplace in Tashbaan, contaminated by their near-
ness to "unwashed people, unwashed dogs . . . and the piles of
refuse." The "no-garlic-please-we're-British" phenomenon was a
very late Victorian development that took a good while to be
shaken off, and there was also a general lack of experience with
the more Mediterranean cuisines. Lewis didn't get down that
way himself until rather late in life, and the at-home-British take
on such food was pretty desperate until the great English food
writer Elizabeth David came along and started showing people
how to get it right. Either way, the "foreign" Calormene food

never really compares positively to the Narnian, which is largely based on historical (or recent-memory) British cooking. You have to wonder what Lewis would have made of the modern Britain, where the number one favorite dish is chicken tikka masala.

There is also, as a side issue, the moment that tells you that whatever a Narnian might think of Calormene food, the Calormenes take it seriously: the Tisroc—having previously pardoned one of his chefs—rather callously recalls the pardon as he feels indigestion coming on after his ultra-secret tête-à-tête with his Vizier and the inflammable Prince Rabadash. Anyone reading the chapter would be inclined to think that the indigestion was more situational than dietary . . . but then we're told straight out that the Calormenes are a cruel people, so maybe nothing better should be expected.

Whatever the case, when Shasta and Aravis and the Horses finally make it into Archenland, the change in tone of the language about food makes it plain where Lewis's preferences lay. The goat's milk (even though it comes as something of a shock to Aravis) and the porridge and cream for breakfast are a hint, and the later meal the Dwarfs give Shasta—the toast and butter (there it is again, with the additional note that Shasta has no idea what it is because "in Calormen you nearly always get oil instead of butter"), the bacon and eggs and mushrooms and coffee—all tell us that we are back in Normal Food Country, and the author is glad to be there.

But the Calormene food is more slighted than actively scorned. What Lewis does *not* bother concealing his scorn for is the kind of "crank" vegetarianism that was beginning to be practiced in Britain postwar. One hopes he was actually reacting to the somewhat insufferable attitude that seems to have gone with the practice at that time, and which he caricatures when describing Eustace Scrubb's "very up-to-date and advanced" mother and father. The "Plumptree's Vitaminized Nerve Food" that Eustace demands after being dropped in the ocean next to the *Dawn Treader*—and that he demands be made with distilled water—gets short shrift.

And there's no arguing with Lewis's condemnation of *ersatz* foods, the less-than-desirable substitutes that were frequently forced on unhappy consumers during the rationing years. The simple sausage would be one example of a food that repeatedly turns up transfigured in the Narnia books. Though sausages weren't rationed during or after wartime, the meat that went into them was, so their desperately padded-out contents would have become a cruel mockery for a man raised in a part of the world whose great culinary claim to fame was the Ulster Fry, a dish incomplete without good sausages. The "hissing . . . and delicious" sausages that Jill and Eustace are given by their Narnian rescuers after their return from inner-earth are a straightforward antidote to the ones Lewis would have had to put up with for at least the previous decade: "not wretched sausages half full of bread and soya bean, either, but real meaty, spicy ones, fat and piping hot and burst and just the tiniest bit burnt."

The annoyed descriptions of food gone wrong, however, are in the minority. Lewis's fondness for a good meal and his willingness to describe it until the reader can practically taste it show up again and again. So does his playfulness about Narnian food. Another writer might sometimes be tempted to think that Lewis is inserting food "business" in one spot or another as a comfort measure, to break the tension of a scene just past. But sometimes these foodie episodes look more like something that

Lewis allowed to happen primarily to amuse himself. And occasionally, during one of these, it's possible to spot the symptoms of an author suddenly thinking through some aspect of his own creation that he hadn't considered until just then. One of these moments is the rather harried description in *The Silver Chair* of the logistics of having a centaur for an overnight visit at your place—

> A Centaur has a man-stomach and a horse-stomach. And of course both want breakfast. So first of all he has porridge and pavenders and kidneys and bacon and omelette and cold ham and toast and marmalade and coffee and beer. And after that he attends to the horse part of himself by grazing for an hour or so and finishing up with a hot mash, some oats and a bag of sugar. That's why it's such a serious thing to ask a Centaur to stay for the weekend. A very serious thing indeed.

—especially in a country where one comfort for the serious cook is definitely missing: the dishwasher. It's a pity that Narnia is, by and large, so resolutely anti-machine. But even the Dwarfs who feed Shasta after his long run to warn the Archenlanders of the impending Calormene invasion describe the one of them who gets picked to do the dishes afterward as "the loser."

Something else amusing turns up in that passage about the Centaur: one of the very few foods that Lewis "invented" for Narnia. This is the pavender, which may be a Narnian-ized version of that uniquely Northern Irish fish, the pollan—a herring-like fresh-water fish related to the Arctic cisco, which like its cousin can only be found in formerly glaciated lakes like Loch Neagh.

Interestingly, Lewis may be punning here, since the word "pavender" isn't unique to him. It appears in exactly one other piece of literature—St. Leger's quirky little poem "The Chavender." The poem is itself an extended wordplay:

> There is a fine stuffed chavender
> A chavender or chub,
> That decks the rural pavender,
> The pavender or pub,
> Wherein I eat my gravender,
> My gravender, or grub.

Lewis almost certainly knew this poem: and he might even have known that the "chavender or chub" was a relative of the pollan—or just looked a whole lot like it—and thought it would be funny to use "pavender" as the Narnian fish's name.

But the fun-and-games approach to Narnian food is not universal in the books, or unmixed with other influences or motivations. There is one notable spot where the humor about food abruptly becomes edgy. Again, this occurs in *The Silver Chair* when Jill, Eustace, and Puddleglum the Marsh-wiggle are staying with the (so-called) Gentle Giants at Harfang. They're in the kitchen waiting for the cook-giantess who's guarding them to fall asleep, and Jill, though not particularly interested in the gigantic open cookbook on the counter, has a look at it. Under the entry for MALLARD, she goes into shock on seeing—

> MAN. This elegant little biped has long been valued as a delicacy. It forms a traditional part of the Autumn Feast, and is served between the fish and the joint. Each Man—

We know from Lewis's letters that he read and often enjoyed the "pulp" science fiction magazines of the period. *The Silver Chair* was published in 1953, and it's difficult to believe that Lewis had not seen Damon Knight's instant-classic SF story, "To Serve Man," when it first appeared in *Galaxy* magazine in 1950. In this story, seemingly friendly aliens turn up to help humanity with its problems, and are almost universally trusted until someone succeeds in translating their "great book," which shares the story's name. This book turns out to be a cookbook, and the aliens not nearly so altruistic as they'd seemed. The trope has since turned up in many other places, especially in film and TV, the story itself most famously appearing as an episode of the original *Twilight Zone*—and it looks as if Lewis was here one of the very first to invoke it for the joke's sake, though the humor is fairly dark.

Much more unsettlingly, though, this is also one of the places where food briefly—and unusually for Lewis—becomes a horror, an occasion of sin, or both. Earlier, just briefly, Edmund's disastrous encounter with Jadis's magical Turkish Delight in *The Lion, the Witch and the Wardrobe* leaves him much more likely to betray his sisters and brother than he would have been had he never eaten any: "Anyone who had once tasted it would want more and more of it, and would even, if they were allowed, go on eating it till they killed themselves." That was bad enough—though Edmund's addiction and treachery did eventually lead to the end of Winter and the death of the Witch. And for his part in this, Edmund is eventually forgiven. But in *The Silver Chair*, when Jill, Eustace, and Puddleglum discover that the venison they've been eating is from a Talking Stag, the horror is inescapable; the sense of helpless anguish among the three of them is crushing. Even at the end of the book, when all seems to be forgiven, there is a lingering sense that forgiveness may still not be enough.

But this level of darkness, whether or not it involves food, is rare in the Narnia books. What are much more common are flashes or hints of deeper meaning hidden inside the outer semblances of the food—beneath the gleam of the salmon, as it were, or more like the light seen through the wine than the wine itself. And though much has been said about what religious symbolism might or might not be hiding (or hidden) behind the characters and situations in the Narnia books, a broader issue sometimes gets pushed off to one side: how the novels might express the way Lewis felt about how religion could interact and coexist with everyday life. Lewis loved the physical world of the five senses as much as he loved the world of the "inner sense" of faith: for him they were part of a seamless continuum. He didn't mind mocking (though genially enough) those who unwisely insisted that the divine could only be truly encountered mentally or spiritually—as if any possible physical experience of God was somehow inferior, and the spiritual kind of experience was somehow purer or better just because it wasn't stuck inside matter.

Yet a motif that turns up again and again in Lewis's work, especially in *The Great Divorce*, is the concept that physical things can't become what they're really intended to be until they come to grips with the divine, surrender to it by way of some kind of death, and are afterward raised or reborn. Even food can manage this to someone of Lewis's beliefs. All the food has to do is become, or be made, part of a sacrament—the matter of bread and wine, of the private feast in the upper room, where the incarnate God sits down with His fellow man and breaks bread in a meal intended to be forever repeated as a sign of their new agreement.

In this light, the table where everybody sits down together to eat becomes a tremendously important symbol suggesting how the material and the spiritual can get along, day by day. And this symbol repeats, in various forms, all over Narnia. The clearest restatement of the theme lies on the table near the edge of the world where the retired star Ramandu and his daughter keep watch over the Stone Knife that once killed Aslan. The presence of the Knife makes the table an echo of another Table, a broken one, and it thereby becomes more than just a platform for one more feast, no matter how wonderfully the meat pies are made to look like ships under sail. Something more profound is going on for the willing viewer, or diner, to see.

A little more examination shows that at all the truly great moments in Narnia—the passages that Tolkien would have described as "eucatastrophe," great and moving change for the good—there is always food around, more or less sauced with symbol. The Tree with its ineffable and miraculous fruit is there at the end of *The Magician's Nephew* and again at the climax of *The Last Battle*—those fruits compared to which "the freshest grapefruit you've ever eaten was dull, and the juiciest orange was dry, and the most melting pear was hard and woody . . . and there were no seeds or stones, and no wasps." The Lamb is there with its breakfast of fresh fish (perhaps pavenders again? Lewis doesn't specify) at the end of *Dawn Treader*. There is the splendor of the great feast in Cair Paravel at the pre-climax of *The Lion, the Witch and the Wardrobe*, with its revelry and dancing, "where gold flashed and wine flowed"; the cold-weather delights of the Winter Feast at which Prince Rilian returns to his people at the end of *The Silver Chair*; and the poem-adorned feast at the end of *The Horse and his Boy* when Prince Cor—the former Shasta—discovers that his destiny is to be King of the land he's saved.

All these occurrences—and, some might say, every occurrence of food in the Narnia books—either openly or secretly restate another theme that Lewis came back to again and again: food as a gift of the divine to men. Somewhere in his later religious writings, Lewis says that the taste and experience of food is one of the manifest signs that God likes us—because (paraphrasing here) almost all the things He has made it necessary for human beings to do to survive are *enjoyable*. And maybe here we hear a late echo of his relationship with his beloved wife, a lady raised in the Jewish tradition, who may have told him about the Mishnaic tradition that after death, God will ask each human being why they were offered interesting or wonderful foods and failed to eat them—because these foods were made by God specifically as a present for humanity.

But this is deep stuff, and Lewis would have been the first to agree that we are not meant to spend all our time in the depths. Sometimes what you really want is to be sitting out in the summer sunshine on some terrace at Anvard or some grassy meadow in the shadow of the orchard outside the gates of Cair Paravel, lunching lightly with friendly royalty on a collation of cold fowl and cold game pies and cheese and wine and bread (always the wine and bread seem to wind up on the table). And at such times, for maximum refreshment of the spirit, only Narnia will do.

Diane Duane is a native Manhattanite who has been living in Ireland for more than twenty years with her husband, novelist and screenwriter Peter Morwood. Diane has been reading science fiction and fantasy since she was eight, and writing it professionally since she was twenty-seven. She's written for characters as diverse as Jean-Luc Picard, Batman, Sigurd the Volsung, and Scooby-Doo, besides writing nine novels in her own Young Wizards universe and more than forty other novels. She was born in a Year of the Dragon, her favorite food is a weird Swiss scrambled-potato dish called *maluns*, and her sign is "Runway 24 Left, Hold For Clearance."

What makes a proper girl? When C. S. Lewis wrote his books, society said she should be "obedient, demure, and in perpetual need of protection." So how come his heroines were anything but? Kelly McClymer tells all in a striking analysis of a woman's place in Narnia.

◆·)⊙·※·⊙(·◆

Serious Action Figures

Girl Power in the Chronicles of Narnia

KELLY MCCLYMER

When I was a child, I never thought much about who wrote the books I loved. I read for the characters, the story, the settings so different from my suburban life. Because most of my books came from library shelves, I considered the librarians as the keepers of the hallowed books. If I'd cared to think about it, I might have assumed those librarians performed magic during the hours between dark and dawn when the library was closed and dark—a special kind of magic that filled the shelves with books of different shapes, colors, sizes, and smells. After all, those books took me, magically, to faraway lands and worlds I'd never dreamed of.

I learned early that, magic or no, I might accidentally take home a book I didn't like. While I used to be, and still am, a forgiving reader, I prefer books where the characters act like real people. Give me characters that are sensible (if misdirected) and flawed (rather than impossibly good) and I'm happy; give me the opposite, and I'm likely to roll my eyes. Fortunately, eye-rollers were rare. I didn't mind the occasional dud when I so often found myself in the world of the likes of Anne from *Anne of Green Gables* and Meg from *A Wrinkle in Time*.

Eventually I realized the magic of books was connected directly to the author listed on the spine; to my further delight, books next to each other with the same author often meant series. A series meant that I got to spend more time with the characters I liked. I still didn't think too much about the author who had created that series magic for me, but I fell under the spell of those who promised long hours in a world unlike my own. Boy on the cover, girl on the cover, historical setting, fantasy world, it didn't matter to me.

And thus, I came to the Chronicles of Narnia lined up neatly on the library shelf, C. S. Lewis on the spines. Having learned my lesson on previous series, I quickly flipped to the inside page to discover the full number and order of the series. Seven—all there on the shelf. I grabbed them greedily, and began to read the first in the car ride home. *The Lion, the Witch and the Wardrobe*. *What a funny title*, I thought. But who could resist a Lion and a Witch, even if the book did seem to focus on what they were going to be wearing? Not me.

The magic I'd come to expect from reading happened almost instantly when I met the Pevensies. And I was relieved to discover a few pages in that a wardrobe is an old-fashioned name for a big wooden dresser/closet combination. Good. Just like most of the girls in Lewis's series, I'd rather read about a dresser than fashion any day (still would). Especially a magical dresser than would take me to a winter wonderland with a wicked queen, a talking Faun named Tumnus, and a battle fought and won by children just like me.

Though I didn't appreciate it consciously at the time, one of the things that drew me into the books was the fact that Lewis's girls were cast in the hero role, not a supporting role. These girls didn't stand to the side and watch while waiting to be rescued as Wendy did in *Peter Pan*, or as girls did in so many other books I had read. Or worse, dress as and pretend to be men in order to fight the good fight, as Eowyn in Tolkien's Lord of the Rings had to do. No, Lewis's girls walked through wardrobes into other worlds, grabbed glowing rings or jumped into pools or paintings that took them someplace exciting and adventurous and potentially dangerous. These girls were like me and my friends: full of curiosity and interested in exploration. That didn't seem strange at all to me. After all, I grew up in a world where there was ample evidence that women could do anything (dressed as women, not disguised as men), from flying a plane around the world (Amelia Earhart) to running a country (Queen Elizabeth II).

I vaguely recognized that Lewis's girls were different from those of many of the authors I read, but I didn't spend too much time thinking about why back then (it was the 1960s, after all, and everyone was talking about how girls were equal to boys). I just enjoyed the magic of Narnia and the authenticity of his girls. The past (as in the 1920 passage of the 19th Amendment allowing women to vote) seemed as distant as a fairy tale to

me. In Lewis, I'd discovered an author who knew not only the
authentic adventure world of boys, but also of girls. At least,
that's how it felt at the time as I devoured all seven books in
less than a week. I was like the children in the books, like the
narrator: I didn't believe in dressing to impress; I was curious;
I wasn't always good at listening to the rules adults set for me,
which seemed arbitrary and stifling.

Another appealing aspect of the books was the fact that it
was the children (girls even more than boys) who led the way
and the adults who muddled about, often unsure and very
often completely wrong, sometimes from vanity and intellec-
tual snobbery, like Uncle Andrew in *The Magician's Nephew*, and
sometimes with calculating evil, like the Narnian witches. Since
I'd observed in my short life that adults didn't always have the
"right"—or even most logical, sensible, or kind—idea in mind,
I liked reading about other kids who were quite willing to recognize (if silently) the inconsistency or self-deception of the
adults around them. Not to mention girl characters who weren't
obsessed with following the adult advice about being "nice."
Instead, they worried about being valiant, honest, and brave.
Lucy Pevensie does not concern herself with mending torn
hems or cleaning her face. She sets out to free Tumnus the Talking Faun, who has been captured by the White Witch because
he helped Lucy escape Narnia on her first visit.

I related to Lucy, because I knew what it felt like to notice
things and have others react with outright skepticism just
because I was too young to have earned any credibility (although
I never noticed anything as interesting as a portal to another
world in any of our closets, sadly). Lucy has a hard time convincing her older siblings that Narnia is not a sign of mental

illness. I still remember feeling annoyed for her when Edmund ignores her warnings about the evil beneath the White Witch's beauty and the danger in eating the Turkish Delight. I admired her pluck—and worried for her safety—when she and Susan try to revive Aslan after he has been tortured and killed by the White Witch and her minions, rather than sit back and wring their hands helplessly.

It was cool to find girls who were guided by a pragmatic common sense, unless curiosity or an occasional cross mood got the better of them for a moment. Too often, girls in the literature I read were concerned with whether or not they had on the prettiest dress and lecturing the boys around them about behaving well. (I love *Peter Pan*, but can you deny that Wendy might have had a lot more fun if she didn't spend so much time tidying and acting the mother to John, Michael, and the Lost Boys?) In contrast to the overly proper girls in some books, who were focused on the idea of husbands and housework much earlier than I ever was, Polly had my attention the moment she convinced Digory they could explore the empty row house a few doors down by crawling through the eaves of attics in their own houses in *The Magician's Nephew*. Yes, as Digory points out, they could get caught and accused of thievery. But who would want to resist the chance to have adventures with ghosts and haunted houses just because there was a little danger involved? When Polly and Digory miscalculate and end up in Digory's uncle's forbidden study, I held my breath, waiting to see how awful their punishment would be.

Of course, with Lewis, as in real life, the punishments were simply to be borne, secondary to the real adventure the children sensed around every unexplored corner. So when Polly reaches for the rings that Uncle Andrew meanly entices her with? Even though I, like Digory, knew she shouldn't take it, I understood why the glow attracts her so much that she can't resist. I'm not sure I would have resisted, either, despite my real fear that Polly would be harmed by whatever was going to happen next. I know I didn't resist falling in with any of the adventures that began with *The Lion, the Witch and the Wardrobe* and ended with *The Last Battle*.

Returning to Lewis's work as an adult has meant indulging in research. I have long since learned (through many college courses, some lively and some tedious) that the authors I did not concern myself with when I first began reading were the true purveyors of the magic I've always found in books. Not only that, but studying their lives often reveals some of the history that shaped and informed the magic worlds they created to delight their readers. Authors, it turned out, take bits and pieces of their real lives to breathe life into their characters and settings. Dickens's all too real experience with a London poorhouse, Twain's life on the Mississippi river and his experience growing up in Missouri before and after the battle to end slavery was finally won—the authors turned out to be characters as interesting as those they created on the page. In turn, the characters they created became more real when I learned how much they shared with their creators in experience. But I had not studied Lewis's history. Would knowing him better make me enjoy the Chronicles of Narnia more? Or less?

I confess to being apprehensive about re-reading the books. What if the magic I'd found in them as a child was ruined by the revelation of the author behind the story? What if the strong girl characters I remembered were not quite as strong as I'd thought?

Fortunately, I came away more in awe of his carefully drawn girl characters than ever.

I am further impressed at how real these girls are because I have now studied the moral, social, and literary pressures that existed from the mid-1600s to the mid-1900s. It was not acceptable—in life or literature—for girls to strive for anything other than absolute perfection in manners and morals (if that sounds boring, it often was, even in literature). Boys like Tom Sawyer could avoid chores and run away to find adventure and still be considered a hero. But girls usually lost their heroic status if they dared to argue, run away, or reject the idea of sitting quietly and waiting for a male to rescue them from trouble. No matter that women waged and won a two-hundred-year war for the right to vote in America and England, and fought for and won the right to own property and businesses in their own right even if they were married; there were still strong forces that argued women were the "weaker" sex.

Authors often found their works better received when the female characters fit the ideal model of womanhood rather than the reality, which led to the depiction of female characters of any age as either completely evil or ridiculously pure, innocent, and helpless. Women were touted in advice and etiquette books as the "angels" of the house. Society expected them to be obedient, demure, and in perpetual need of protection. Authors (male and female) often bowed to the pressure and created such characters (ignoring the real women of their acquaintance, I suspect, who were not nearly so angelically delicate, despite the many etiquette and advice books trying to make them so).

Whatever history, religious leanings, or meanings Lewis held, he never let them obscure his accurate observation of the behavior of the girls in his books. That makes Lewis a little different from his contemporaries like Tolkien and American classicists like Mark Twain (who preferred to use female characters as sparingly as possible, and then only in supporting roles). Where Tolkien and Twain created strong and memorable male characters in Frodo Baggins, Samwise Gamgee, Tom Sawyer, and Huck Finn, they did not cast, as Lewis did, equally strong females as protagonists. Think of it in terms of whether you can imagine one of today's enterprising toy companies turning the characters into action figures: While Frodo, Sam, Tom, and Huck can all be easily seen as action figure worthy, can the same be said for Becky Thatcher, with her golden hair and concerns about boyfriends and kissing? Contrast that with all seven of the books in the Chronicles of Narnia. Every girl, beginning with Lucy Pevensie opening the wardrobe and discovering Narnia in *The Lion, the Witch and the Wardrobe*, and ending with Jill Pole discovering and protecting the fake Aslan in *The Last Battle*, acts, reacts, makes mistakes, and proves herself as a hero worthy of her own action figure.

In fact, Lucy and Susan already have action figures, thanks to the Disney movie version of *The Lion, the Witch and the Wardrobe*. I would have dressed Lucy and Susan more practically for their action figures (hard to fight in flowing skirts), but I'd have given them the same accessories (Lucy has her healing cordial, while Susan carries her bow and arrows and her horn). For the others: Jill Pole is easiest—she'd be in Calormene armor (or maybe a Girl Guide uniform) and have a bow and arrow. Polly would carry the rings—one green and one yellow—and have a pair of gloves to protect herself from their magic. Aravis would be in armor, with a sword—and her Talking Horse Hwin, of course. The action figures of these girls would be a far cry from the first Barbie (who was created right around the same time Lewis was writing the Narnia books, as it happens).

It is only now, upon reflection on the history of women's rights and literature of the times, that I realize how lucky I was that Lewis wrote girls who could inspire me so well. Although Lucy is a close second, Jill Pole remains my favorite action girl of Narnia. She isn't as arrogant as Aravis, but she is as brave and strong. As a character in the later books, toward the end of the Narnian cycle, Jill can be seen as the perfection of the über-unprissy (and yet not masculine) girl character that Lewis began crafting with Lucy Pevensie. In the final book, *The Last Battle*, she states her mind, isn't afraid to disobey the orders of a king to uncover the secret of the fake Aslan, and—unlike Susan Pevensie in *The Lion, the Witch and the Wardrobe*—she wields her bow and arrows proficiently to help save Narnia in a fierce and dangerous battle. To be fair, Susan does get to use her bow in a battle (of sorts) against the Dwarf Trumpkin in *Prince Caspian*. But Jill's arrows fly true and strike down many enemies in the heat of battle when the fate of Narnia is at stake.

So how did the author behind the curtain of the Chronicles of Narnia come to know the minds and hearts of girls so well? After all, his mother died when he was ten, he had no sisters, and he was sent to a boarding school shortly after his mother died, where he spent a great deal of his time in the company of boys and men. Not to mention that he didn't marry until late in life. And yet he (much better than Tolkien in his fantasy universe) understood the character of his Narnian girls and authentically drew their faults and their strengths. Where did he learn about the power of girls?

My guess is that he observed people—all kinds of people, from girls to women and boys to men. Finely drawn characters that ring true to life are usually the result of an author who observes the world and people around him keenly. And then, instead of bowing to literary convention that preferred female characters be portrayed as stereotypically good or evil, he put real girls on the page to delight young readers of both genders.

Having read a little of his many letters, which seem to be silent on this point, I am left to wonder whether he portrayed his females authentically because it did not occur to him to do otherwise (despite the fact that his contemporary and close friend Tolkien chose otherwise), or whether he was striking a blow for the rights that he had been watching women fight for and win all of his life. It was easy for me, as a child, to overlook the earth-shattering nature of the changes that occurred in society when women began to claim the right to full citizenship. (My study of history corrected that impression of "easy," natural change when I learned that Abigail Adams had implored her husband to give women the vote back when he was working with others to craft the new country of the United States, over a century before women finally did get the vote.) Lewis, on the other hand, was a young man in Ireland when these important battles were raging in the newspaper and in each home. How much did this battle affect his characters? Comparing the history going on around him with the events in his novels, there are many easy connections to make.

Lewis served in World War I, and his battle scenes, as well as those scenes where wearily embattled characters seek shelter and make do with little food, reflect the realities of war. But war was for men at that time, so where might he have observed women on a battlefield or suffering the realities of too little food and inadequate shelter? History reveals that WWI and WWII were periods when professional nursing was finally blossoming into a career to be respected and revered, as these women worked to save wounded soldiers from dying of infection and fever. Nurses, almost exclusively female, were at the front lines, hardy and brave. Lucy, with her healing potion, and Susan, with her motherly caution, can be seen as reflections of those strong, brave women.

Lewis grew up in an era when women were fighting for, and finally winning, the right to vote in England and America. No observant, thinking man of his era could sit back and conceive of women as soft, brainless creatures. And yet the literature of the time often hesitated to portray even the "good" female characters as anything but angels—or future angels—of the house, a Victorian-period notion that hung on long past the death of Queen Victoria in 1901. Lewis was clearly an observant, thinking man; we can tell as much from his writing. While he still gives the bulk of his combat to the men and boys that people the Chronicles of Narnia, he does not sideline the girls nor saddle them with the responsibility of being mother hens who lecture about goodness and propriety and worry most about keeping their hands clean and their voices down. No, Lucy opens the wardrobe, has an adventure all on her own, and shows her older, reluctant, doubtful siblings how to follow her to save Tumnus (and eventually Narnia itself). In *The Magician's Nephew*, Polly not only leads Digory on the trek through the attic, but her common sense often keeps them on a sensible course even while they both eagerly satisfy their curiosity about the new world they find themselves in (if only Digory had lis-

tened when Polly told him not to ring the bell!). The girls are as
smart, curious, brave, and flawed as any of the boys.

Another historical reality in Lewis's world was the shift of
women out of the home and into the workplace to support the
war effort in WWII. Rosie the Riveter was a model for women
here in the U.S. who manned the factory jobs while the men
were away at war. Lewis's girls aren't afraid to don armor and
wield swords when they must do so for the cause, either.

Lastly, and most explicitly, Lewis gives a nod to England's
Girl Guides when Eustace explains to King Tirian in *The Magician's Nephew* that Jill Pole's tracking abilities come from her
years as a Guide. The ability to move silently (startling friend
as much as enemy) and track her route by the stars of Narnia
allows Jill to lead King Tirian's party, not just follow along in
the wake of the men and boys. It seems unlikely that Lewis did
this unconsciously. I suspect he made his decisions deliberately,
given his life as a Cambridge scholar. After all, the boys and
men (and Talking Animals) do not question Jill's leadership or
abilities just because she is a girl (when even in modern-day life
that still happens—if less frequently).

It wasn't just the good female characters who were strong,
fearless, and daring, either. As a child, I did not find it strange
that one of the prime villains in Narnia is female. The Witch
was as believable to me as any other larger-than-life villain.
After all, I'd grown up with the Disney versions of Cinderella,
Snow White, and Sleeping Beauty. What was wrong with an evil
Witch in a land of Talking Animals?

However, Lewis's Witch is not merely cunning and devi-
ous—she is a bombshell beautiful giant with the strength to
pull street lamps out of the ground and smack policemen with

them. The actions of Jadis the Witch in *The Magician's Nephew* are both breathtakingly cruel (as when she leaves her people in suspended animation and lets the castle crumble and collapse around them because they are her people to destroy or save) and astonishingly funny (as when she runs the cab and horse to the ground while being chased by police and distraught jewelers). Her physical and magical powers are more than a match for any man, in Narnia or in England.

Though the destruction of her own world reduces her powers, she is still powerful as the White Witch in *The Lion, the Witch and the Wardrobe*. In that book she is still beautiful enough to charm Edmund Pevensie (as she had Uncle Andrew in *The Magician's Nephew*) and heartless enough to bring endless winter to Narnia without allowing the relief of Christmas. It takes Aslan, the great Lion-creator of Narnia himself, to vanquish her in the end, as her power is greater than any boy, king, or Talking Beast of Narnia can overcome. Although one may note that the girls, Lucy, Susan, and Polly, quickly see through to her cold black heart. They are not fooled by beauty as Edmund and Uncle Andrew are.

Sadly, there is one girl Lewis barred from his Narnia in the final volume, *The Last Battle*—Susan Pevensie, one of Narnia's first defenders and its former queen, Queen Susan the Gentle. Despite her battles at the side of her younger siblings in *The Lion, the Witch and the Wardrobe*, and at the side of Prince Caspian in *Prince Caspian*, Susan has turned away from Narnia, choosing to believe it was a childish game of fantasy and make-believe. Instead, to everyone's great scorn, she has embraced "nylons and lipsticks and invitations," as Jill Pole says in *The Final Battle*. Some have argued this shows Lewis's misogyny, but after seven books where all the girls play major roles (remember—action figures with armor and weapons) and only one of the girls—the one who has denied the existence of Narnia—is left behind, I'd have to disagree.

Instead, I'd argue that Lewis was simply emphasizing his point that characters who turn away from honor and valor and duty for the frivolities of life cannot see or enter Narnia. After all, he made his disdain for fancy dress plain in every book— my favorite example occurs in *The Magician's Nephew*, when the cabbie's wife Helen, who becomes the first Queen of Narnia, is summoned into Narnia by Aslan. She appears in her apron and the narrator comments she'd have put on her good clothes had she known he'd be spirited out of her world but would have looked the worse for it. At ten, I agreed with this sentiment— and I still do, several decades later.

When I read the books as a child, I knew nothing of Lewis the author. I knew only the characters and adventures on the page. I had fought with them, taken sides in their quarrels, held my breath when they took risks that didn't seem wise, and released sighs of relief when they came through their scrapes stronger, better, and wiser than before. When I closed the cover of *The Last Battle*, I had complete faith that Susan would eventually redeem herself and get to Narnia again. After all, she had been a Queen of Narnia and had been gentle and wise. She had fought bravely and won the battle once against her own desire to be "grown-up" in the way that Lewis and his characters despised. Surely she could do so again.

I have since been heartened to learn that others feel the same. Susan, after all, does not die in the train accident as the others do (thus allowing their ultimate transition from Narnia to the far eastern land of Aslan's father, the Emperor-over-the-Sea). She lives in the "real" world, sure that Narnia was only a childhood game. Lewis makes clear in his books that there are other ways to reach Aslan's land—sailing to the end of the Silver Sea, for example—even after Aslan has turned the land of Narnia into a great sea at the end of *The Last Battle*. Susan, with her lipstick and nylons and concern about invitations, is too smart to forever embrace the Victorian fallacy of the "angel in the house." I have faith that, by the end of her life, Susan will have re-embraced the magical and vibrant world of authentic girls that Lewis created and find her way to Aslan's land. In my perfect world, she does, at last, reclaim the courage, honor, and valor—the magic—and abandon the lipstick and nylons. After all, she's got her own action figure, doesn't she?

⊸⊱⊰⊱※⊰⊱⊰⊸

Kelly McClymer has been a reader and a writer for as long as she can remember. The world of books offered so much to her growing up that she feels lucky to have given back with her own somewhat twisted imagination-fueled novels. Her list of books for young adults includes *Getting to Third Date* and the fantasy trilogy *The Salem Witch Tryouts*, *Competition's a Witch*, and *She's a Witch Girl*. Her latest effort, *Must Love Black*, out in the fall of 2008, is what she terms "goth meets gothic on the coast of Maine."

His Dark Materials *author Philip Pullman famously described the Chronicles of Narnia as "ugly and poisonous." Other no less violent critics claim C. S. Lewis was a racist. But could it not be argued that Lewis was just a child of his time? Lisa Papademetriou makes the analysis and concludes the answer is more complex than it might seem.*

◆•▷▶◈◀◁•◆

In the Kingdom of Calormen

LISA PAPADEMETRIOU

When I sat down to re-read *The Horse and His Boy*, I felt a familiar thrill of excitement. I was ten years old when I discovered the Narnia books. I read them obsessively—at least thirteen times each—and *The Horse and His Boy* was always one of my favorites. As a young reader, I was delighted by the view of Narnia from a different angle, and the surprise of re-encountering Lucy, Edmund, and Susan during the time of their reign. I vaguely remembered being entranced by the descriptions of Calormen, and of Calormene society. This assignment seemed like the perfect opportunity to re-read the book and take a closer look.

Unfortunately, I wasn't happy with everything I saw. Oh, the storytelling was just as beautiful as I recalled and the plot was exciting. And I still loved the characters—Shasta and Bree, Hwin and Aravis. But I was surprised and dismayed to come across a few extremely cringe-worthy descriptions of the people and culture of Arab-inspired Calormen that I didn't remember from my youth. Part of the issue is undoubtedly that I was reading the book during a different time in my life, but part of it was just as undoubtedly that I was reading the book during a different time period—the 2000s, not the 1980s. The context in which I originally read the books has changed.

Lewis's intent in creating the Calormene Empire is the subject of much debate. Some scholars have attacked Lewis as a racist and claimed he was hostile to religions and cultures different from his own. Others have defended him, claiming that he created Calormene characters to show that people of other races can still be good and noble. However, no matter what you believe Lewis meant, there is no doubt that our current era has influenced the way in which his work is read, making the things he says about the Muslim world seem both more relevant and—in some cases—more objectionable.

Many scholars assume that Lewis intended for Calormen to represent a powerful Islamic country in order to show Islam as Christianity's natural enemy (these scholars believe that Lewis thought of Narnia as an idealized Christian nation). In his book *The Natural History of Make-Believe*, John Goldthwaite writes, "As a Protestant fundamentalist, Lewis liked to ridicule other faiths in his pages, attacking Islam in *The Horse and His Boy*, for example." Gregg Easterbrook refers to the Calormenes as "the principal bad guys" in an *Atlantic Monthly* article about Lewis, and claims that they are "unmistakable Muslim stand-ins." And in *Reading With the Heart* Peter Schakel asserts that the Calormenes are based on the Moors—that is, the Muslims of Spain.

The references to Calormene clothes and physical surroundings support the idea that Calormen represents an Islamic empire. For example, the hero of *The Horse and His Boy*, Shasta, is raised in a Calormene fishing village where the men wear "long, dirty robes, and wooden shoes turned up at the toe, and turbans on their heads, and beards." It is obviously a poor village, which is what makes the appearance of a Tarkaan—or great Calormene lord—all the more striking: "The spike of a helmet projected from the middle of his silken turban, and he wore a shirt of chain mail. By his side hung a curving scimitar. . . ." These details—the robes, the turned-up shoes, the turbans, the scimitar—are doubtless meant to evoke Arabia and the Persian Empire. When the books were released in the 1950s, many young readers would have been familiar with the descriptions of these fashions from the pages of *One Thousand and One Nights*, also known as *Arabian Nights*, a popular book based on fairy tales and fantasies from Persia, Arabia, and India. Today's readers are more likely to recognize the descriptions from the Disney movie *Aladdin*—which is based on an *Arabian Nights* tale. Either way, these details do reflect some historical and contemporary Muslim fashions: Arabians wear long robes; Pakistanis wear *khussas* (shoes turned up at the toe); the scimitar is a traditional weapon in Arabia, Persia, and Turkey; and fabric head coverings (including the turban) are common all over the Islamic world. In addition, the architecture of the capital city, Tashbaan, is clearly Islamic in style: it includes "balconies, deep archways, pillared colonnades, spires, battlements, minarets, pinnacles." Minarets, for example, are onion-shaped spires found on mosques, or Islamic temples.

The Calormenes have a very distinct style of speech and storytelling, which is also vaguely Islamic. Whenever a character invokes the title of the Tisroc (the Calormene emperor), the word is always followed by the parenthetical phrase, "may he live forever." This is reminiscent of Islamic invocations of the prophet Mohammed, which are always followed by "peace be upon him." Lewis says that, in Calormen, storytelling is an art— one that is actually taught in schools. When Shasta asks Aravis, *The Horse and His Boy*'s heroine, for her backstory, she tells it "in the grand Calormene manner." Both the style of her tale and the flowery Calormene speech are also reminiscent of *Arabian Nights*.

The evidence certainly seems to suggest that Lewis meant for Calormen to remind his readers of the Muslim people and culture. And yet, in one very important way, Calormen is clearly not representative of Islam. Muslims are monotheistic. They worship one all-powerful God, which is the same as the Judeo-Christian god of Abraham found in the Old Testament. The Calormenes—by contrast—are polytheistic, which means that they worship several gods. The main Calormene god is the bird-headed demon Tash, the "irresistible, the inexorable," but other, lesser gods and goddesses are named as well. Aravis talks of the goddess Zardeenah, to whom girls must make sacrifices on the eve of their marriage. If Lewis had wanted to make a mockery of the Islamic religion, wouldn't he have created a Calormene faith that was at least recognizably close to the original?

So why would Lewis bother to create a clearly Muslim-inspired world if he didn't actually wish to portray Muslims?

Part of the issue is the form Lewis chose for his Narnia stories—a form he terms a fairy tale. As he says in his book of essays *Of Other Worlds*: "I fell in love with the Form itself: its brevity, its severe restraints on description, its flexible traditionalism, its inflexible hostility to analysis, digression, reflections, and 'gas.'" Lewis wanted readers to respond to his writing with their guts, not their minds. He often chose characters and settings that felt familiar in order to let the readers fill in the blanks with their own associations. The details and descriptions of the Muslim-inspired Calormenes—flowing robes, scimitars, and all—are intended to evoke an emotional response in the reader. For readers in the 1950s, Calormene society would have seemed strange and foreign—any reader familiar with the *Arabian Nights* would have thought of the Calormenes as mysterious, exotic, and perhaps even magical—and that alone was enough to make the reader uneasy and underline the sense of danger that our heroes are in. (Today's readers are likely to find the Calormenes additionally threatening, since our media is full of stories about Islamic fundamentalism and terrorism.) This was clearly done very deliberately. In his essay "On Stories," Lewis makes the distinction between readers who enjoy stories for plot, and those for whom the experience is heightened by these sorts of atmospheric details. It is mood that Lewis is after:

> If to love Story is to love excitement then I ought to be the greatest lover of excitement alive. But the fact is that what is said to be the most "exciting" novel in the world, *The Three Musketeers*, makes no appeal to me at all. The total lack of atmosphere repels me.

Lewis chose to fill *The Horse and His Boy* with atmosphere. Yet he wished to accomplish this without lengthy descriptions that would distract the reader from the excitement of the advancing story. Lewis's choice of the fairy tale form to do this is both a strength and a weakness. It is a strength in that his brief descriptions of the Calormenes and their country are powerfully effective—for Lewis's anticipated readership the descriptions were exotic, and in the new post–September 11 era they are both exotic and frightening. But the choice of the fairy tale form is a weakness in that sometimes these descriptions are so brief that they cross the line into stereotypes. In order to be effective they call upon the reader's worst assumptions about the "otherness" of Islamic people. Calormene society is meant to seem very different from the reader's world and from Narnia. While Lewis means readers to see Narnians as being "like us" (they even celebrate Christmas despite the fact that Jesus never existed in Narnia), the Calormenes—and by associations, Muslims—seem "not like us" in negative ways. Lewis's contrast between Narnians and Calormenes undoubtedly resonates even more strongly with today's readers, who are used to seeing images of radical Muslims and hearing that they are the enemies of freedom—just as Calormene culture frequently threatens the Narnian way of life.

Lewis compounds the issue by often contrasting Calormen with Narnia in an effort to show the superiority of Narnian values. For example, the Calormene culture is highly hierarchical and concerned with class (who has the highest status and the most power) and money. In the country's capital—Tashbaan—"there is only one traffic regulation, which is that everyone who is less important has to get out of the way for everyone who

is more important." When Prince Rabadash kicks the Grand
Vizier, his father, the Tisroc, tells him, "even as a costly jewel
retains its value if hidden in a dung-hill, so old age and discre-
tion are to be respected even in the vile persons of our subjects."
Clearly, the Tisroc does not feel much respect for his own people . . . even high-ranking advisors.

Narnians, on the other hand, are extremely egalitarian. The
Narnian kings and queens travel with and take counsel from
Talking Animals, viewing them as equal to themselves. In Narnia, honesty, bravery, and self-sacrifice matter much more than
social class—it is, after all, a place where a Talking Mouse can
become a great hero. When Shasta spots a band of Narnians
in the city of Tashbaan, the first thing he notes is that none of
them is riding in a litter—which means, of course, that there
are no slaves among them. Instead, they are on foot and dressed
in bright colors. "And instead of being grave and mysterious
like most Calormenes, they walked with a swing and let their
arms and shoulders go free, and chatted and laughed. One was
whistling. You could see that they were ready to be friends with
anyone who was friendly and didn't give a fig for anyone who
wasn't." The Narnians pluck Shasta out of the crowd and drag
him along with them because they are so clueless about social
class that they can't tell the difference between a poor uned-
ucated boy from a fishing village and their compatriot Corin,
Prince of Archenland.

Sometimes these contrasts seem to cross a line into racism.
There is no denying that there are some extremely uncomfort-
able descriptions of the Calormenes in the Chronicles of Narnia—especially the ones that emphasize the skin color of the
Calormenes. The Calormenes are repeatedly described as uglier

than their Narnian counterparts due to their dark complexions. For example, when the Tarkaan comes to Shasta's village and offers to buy him as a slave from his so-called father, he notes: "This boy is manifestly no son of yours, for your cheek is as dark as mine but the boy is fair and white like the accused but beautiful barbarians who inhabit the remote North."[1] Even when Lewis tries to be complimentary, he can't help coming off as patronizing. In describing Emeth, the noble and good Calormene in *The Last Battle*, he writes, "He was young and tall and slender, and even rather beautiful in the dark, haughty, Calormene way." What a qualification! Why not simply end the sentence after the word "beautiful?" Finishing it the way Lewis does implies that the white Western standard of beauty—the Narnian standard—is the universal ideal, and that Calormenes are to be held to a different standard.

Lewis wasn't very kind when describing the Calormenes' odors, either. He refers to their breath as smelling of garlic and onions. The great capital city of Tashbaan is positively ripe with odors: "What you would chiefly have noticed if you had been there was the smells, which came from unwashed people, unwashed dogs, scent, garlic, onions, and the piles of refuse which lay everywhere." Even in heaven, the talking dogs of Narnia manage to sniff out Emeth as a Calormene: "Anyone can

---

[1] I feel the need to point out that, in *The Last Battle*, the Dwarfs call their Calormene captors "Darkies," which is a term that has historically been used to refer—negatively—to people with dark skin. But as Gregg Easterbrook has pointed out, the group of Dwarfs who use the epithets in that book are the vilest creatures in the history of Narnia. Even a very young reader would understand not to respect anything they say, so when they call the Calormenes racist names, it says more about the Dwarfs than it does about the Calormenes.

smell what *that* is." Not the most flattering portrait. All this is meant to call up stereotypes about foreign cooking and exotic scents. It is interesting to note, though, that as a result of globalization, especially the exposure to other cultures' foods, the smell of garlic and onions has a great deal more appeal now than it would have had in mid-twentieth-century England. Lewis thought of these smells as exotic and unpleasant, whereas today's reader would find them very common.

But these unflattering descriptions are not all there is to the Calormene argument. Lewis also presents the reader with a couple of characters clearly intended to bring a personal perspective to life in Calormen: Aravis (of *The Horse and His Boy*) and Emeth (of *The Last Battle*). Both of these characters are presented as "good" Calormenes, and are often cited as evidence that the books aren't racist at all. But what does it really mean to be a "good" Calormene?

When Aravis is first introduced in the story, Shasta and his horse Bree hear—but do not see—her riding beside them. Bree can tell right away that the rider is of a superior social class to Shasta: "That's quality, that horse is. And it's being ridden by a real horseman. I tell you what it is, Shasta. There's a Tarkaan under the edge of that wood." Aravis is, of course, not a great Tarkaan warrior at all, but rather a Tarkheena—the daughter of a lord who is descended in a straight line from the god Tash. She is running away from Calormen to escape an arranged marriage to a much older suitor. (Perhaps worst of all—in Calormene terms—this suitor wasn't even born a Tarkaan, but is a commoner who has wormed his way into the Tisroc's favor with "flattery and evil counsels.") Thus she and Shasta find themselves in much the same boat—they are each fleeing Calormen on the back of a Talking Narnian Horse. And yet, Lewis makes it clear that they are not on equal footing. Aravis is cultured and educated, while Shasta suffers from a lifetime of deprivation in a fishing village. She is proud, and constantly reminds Shasta of his lower place in society through both her words and her actions. And yet it is this very society that she claims to want to leave behind, thanks to the injustices it has heaped on her—a desire to escape that seems perfectly natural to today's Western reader, used to hearing about unequal rights for women in some Muslim countries.

Far from being a Calormene stereotype, Aravis is the most interesting, complex character in the entire Narnian cycle (I'll admit it, she was always my favorite). I find it noteworthy those who accuse the Narnian books of being racist and anti-girl always seem to overlook Aravis, who is much smarter than Shasta (a white male Archenlander) and always at least as brave. It is fitting that Shasta and Bree initially mistake her for a warrior. She idolizes her older brother, who died in battle, thinks feminine things are silly, and is unflinchingly fearless. Lewis too seems to admire her courage and loyalty: "She was proud and could be hard enough but she was as true as steel and would never have deserted a companion, whether she liked him or not." When Aravis discovers that she is to be married to Ahoshta Tarkaan, her first inclination is to take her own life. She has no fear of death, preferring it to the gilded cage that she would endure as wife of the future Grand Vizier.

But her mare, Hwin, persuades her to run away to Narnia instead. And so Aravis concocts a complex escape plan that ensures her several days' worth of travel before anyone will even begin looking for her. Shasta, by contrast, doesn't come up with a plan at all, but rather leaves all of the heavy thinking to his Horse, Bree. But her cleverness is, at times, tempered with cruelty and selfishness—as part of her plan, Aravis drugs a maid, knowing full well that the maid will be beaten for allowing Aravis to leave the household alone.

Aravis bucks nearly every Calormene tradition possible. She spurns money and jewels in favor of honor, rejects the feminine ideal, and refuses to obey her parents when they try to force her into marriage. When she runs into her dim-witted friend Lasaraleen in Tashbaan, Lasaraleen is aghast at Aravis's plans. Lasaraleen is a true product of Calormene values, and she doesn't understand why Aravis wouldn't want to marry Ahosta Tarkaan—especially now that he has just been made Grand Vizier. For Lasaraleen, the concept of marrying for love—or even mutual respect—is completely alien. The only proper motivation for marriage (as for all things in Calormene culture) is financial and social gain: "But, darling, only think! Three palaces, and one of them that beautiful one down on the lake at Ilkeen. Positively ropes of pearls, I'm told. Baths of asses' milk. And you'd see such a lot of *me*." Similarly, Lasaraleen is outraged and horrified by the idea that Aravis is traveling with a "peasant boy." In contrast, Shasta rises in Aravis's esteem in this moment, as she realizes that she has more in common with him than with Lasaraleen. Aravis understands that going to Narnia will mean sacrificing her high rank in society, but this doesn't matter to her. Once again, there is her honor—rather than her status—to think of: "I'll be a nobody, just like him, when we get to Narnia. And anyway, I promised."

Another honorable Calormene appears at the end of the Narnian cycle. In *The Last Battle*, Emeth (also a brave and noble

Tarkaan) is the only Calormene in the story who is both devout and brave enough to desire to meet his god, Tash, face to face. When the evil ape, Shift, proclaims that anyone can go into the stable to meet "Tashlan," Emeth alone among Calormenes and Narnians announces that he intends to enter the stable and meet Tash. Knowing the scimitars that wait inside, his Calormene captain tries to talk him out of it, but Emeth is undeterred. And so, he goes inside, and—although he manages to kill the guard placed there—meets his death. Soon after, the entire world is destroyed, and Aslan separates the good from the evil. The good go to Aslan's country, and the evil disappear into a shadow and are never seen again. Emeth is, unsurprisingly, among the good. From this, Lewis defenders have concluded that the book is making a point about universal salvation for those of pure heart.

But are Aravis and Emeth really proof that Lewis wanted to express respect for those of other cultures?

In *Reading with the Heart* Peter J. Schakel points out that Aravis "becomes queen of Archenland when she marries the fair-skinned hero." But the fact that Aravis marries Shasta at the end of the book is actually a double-edged sword. An interracial marriage, by itself, would seem to suggest that Lewis is making a point about good people of different cultures finding common ground. And yet Aravis has from the very beginning of the book rejected everything about her own culture. So what the book really manages to suggest is that the only good Calormene is one who prefers Narnia to Calormen—one who wants to *become* a Narnian.

Similarly, Gregg Easterbrook makes the following point about Emeth:

Emeth ("Truth" in Hebrew) then finds himself in
heaven, being praised by Aslan, and asks why he has
been permitted to enter when in life he worshipped a
rival faith. Aslan tells Emeth that the specifics of religion do not matter; virtue is what's important, and
paradise awaits anyone of good will.

Well . . . that's *sort of* what Aslan says. Actually, when Emeth
tells Aslan that he spent his life in service to Tash, Aslan
replies that every honorable deed done in Tash's name was,
in fact, done for Aslan. This is not because the two deities are
the same, but rather, because they are opposites, "For I and he
are of such different kinds that no service which is vile can be
done to me, and none which is not vile can be done to him."
This sounds so good that one is tempted to overlook the fact
that it doesn't really make much sense. Emeth was raised to
worship and serve Tash. So where did he get his understanding of honor if not from the culture that raised him—a culture that worships Tash? What Aslan is really claiming here is
that one cannot be a true product of Calormene religion and
culture without being horribly corrupted by it. If you are not
corrupt, it is because—deep in your heart—you were really
Narnian all along.

It's interesting to note that "Aslan's country" encompasses
not just Narnia, but further-off places as well, including Tashbaan and even England. One has to wonder about Aslan's
Tashbaan—it must be a very empty place. After all, Emeth is so
unique in heaven that the Narnian dogs sniff him out immediately. One does not get the sense that many Calormenes passed
Aslan's test for entry to heaven.

I have been a fan of C. S. Lewis—and particularly of the Narnia books—for years. And yet I think it is important to read his books carefully and think about what they say in a serious way. Unlike Philip Pullman, I'm not ready to write off the entire series as "ugly and poisonous." It would be useless to do so, anyway; the series is simply too popular and too widely read to disregard. But hopefully we can find a way to challenge the books' assumptions through careful, thoughtful reading, and use them as another way to help us confront our fears and assumptions about Islamic culture. Like much of Lewis's work, the many layers and textures in the Chronicles of Narnia offer an opportunity to see our own world in new, more enlightened ways, both ones Lewis intended, and ones he did not.

<hr />

Lisa Papademetriou is the author of many novels, including *The Wizard, the Witch, and Two Girls from Jersey* (a parody with references to many classic fantasy books such as the Chronicles of Narnia); *Sixth-Grade Glommers, Norks, and Me*; *Chasing Normal*; and *How to Be a Girly-Girl in Just Ten Days*. Her Disney Fairies book, *Rani in the Mermaid Lagoon*, was a *New York Times* bestseller. To find out more about Lisa, check out her website: www.lisapapa.com.

A small girl enters a strange, haunted land where witches once roamed, the inhabitants speak a different tongue, and a weird, wolf-skin coat hangs in a massive wardrobe. . . . Another visit to Narnia? Not quite. For now, as a grown woman, Sophie Masson bewails the loss of two enchanted lands—the one she knew in her real life and the one she came to love through the pen of C. S. Lewis.

————◆‧▸▨‧◈‧◃‧◂‧◆————

Going to Narnia

Sophie Masson

My parents are French, though they worked in many different countries, and when I was a child, we used to go back to France for a long holiday every couple of years, leaving our usual life in Australia behind. We left a world of city bustle and busy roads, English at school, and a suburban Sydney block for a very different one: a beautiful, haunted village house deep in the green southwestern French countryside, not far from an ancient wood which had the reputation of being enchanted. These worlds, and our experiences in them, couldn't have been more different. In Sydney we weren't allowed to venture outside the front gate on our own—our parents being terrified of cars, of strangers, of misadventures of all sorts—while in Empeaux, the quiet village where we lived in France, they relaxed, and we could roam free. We explored up and down the house and ranged over the huge park-like gardens, hung around in the village with the other kids, and took our bikes on long adventures to the woods, the river, or the next village.

Our house in Sydney wasn't very old, though it was older than many in Australia, and we knew every inch of it. Our house in France, with its cellars, attics, passageways, big rooms full of gorgeous old furniture, and resident ghost, seemed an inexhaustible source of wonders and adventures. More than two hundred years old, its outbuildings dated from the Middle Ages, as did the bricked-up well (where, it was reputed, centuries ago a witch had been thrown) and the giant elm tree outside my parents' bedroom window, where owls hooted spookily at night. The house might have had a ghost, but it was also a friendly house—a good-fairy house. Everyone who'd ever lived there loved it and hated to leave it—even the ghost, I expect! Once, when we were in residence there, we got a visit from a lovely old gentleman who used to live there as a child, and who told us it was the only house he saw now in his dreams.

In Sydney we spoke in English, outside the house at least; in France we spoke French, of course. We sometimes attended the village school in Empeaux, and that too was utterly different from our Australian city school: it was small, with all the pupils in one room no matter their grade; in the younger years you used slates and chalk and then graduated to inkwells and blotters and squared writing books, instead of pencils, lined exercise books, and ballpoint pens. French schoolwork was harder and required more learning by heart, more grammar, more attention to handwriting—oh, how hard that was for me and my messy script, I never got the grasp of writing with ink and blotters and always smudged my work! You didn't get to write "compositions" or do creative writing, like you did in Australia; it was all dictation and parsing of paragraphs and analysis of poems. You recited history lessons about "our ancestors the Gauls" and not about Anzacs fighting at Gallipoli. You didn't wear uniforms like in Australia, but just a pinafore over your ordinary clothes. Instead of eating sandwiches in the playground, you got to go home for lunch, where you had two hours off to digest.

Usually we went to France in the spring or summer, but once we went at Christmas. And that was more different. Christmas was always magical for us, because our parents made it so. But it was on an even greater level of magic that year. For the first time in years it snowed in Empeaux for Christmas, and we went to Midnight Mass at the village church with everything glittering like fairyland around us, and then went home to a roaring fire, a tree piled with presents, and even notes from Father Christmas, written in gold ink.

It's not surprising then that I was the sort of child whose reading taste ran mostly to fantasy and especially the kind of fantasy where you go from a "normal" world into an enchanted one. It didn't seem like a fantasy to me; in fact it felt familiar, easy to understand and believe in. It felt natural. When you boarded the plane, you moved from one world to another; once you were in that other world, the one you'd come from might as well not have existed. You forgot about it. It vanished into another dimension. Lots happened to you while you were away, yet when you came back, it seemed as if nothing had happened; your friends were doing just the same things as before, and school went on just the same as ever. And so, when I discovered the Chronicles of Narnia at about age seven or eight, just before going off on one of our family visits back to France, it made perfect sense to me.

In my parents' room in our house in France, there was a huge old wardrobe that looked rather like the picture in *The Lion, the Witch and the Wardrobe*. It too was filled with coats, some of them fur, including a heavy dark wolf-skin coat that my great-grandmother had brought back from Canada, where part of the family came from. As a little kid, I was a bit scared of that coat, which seemed to loom on its big wooden hanger like a giant wolf waiting to spring. I thought it smelled rank, too, like a hibernating beast. After I'd read *The Lion, the Witch and the Wardrobe*, I pushed my way gingerly past it to crawl into the wardrobe and sit there amongst the smell of moth-balls, imagining, with my heart beating a bit faster—what if, when I touched the back of the wardrobe, it suddenly melted away under my touch and I was in that winter Narnia, where it's never Christmas? That it didn't happen didn't matter, not really. I could see it so vividly. I could imagine myself walking out there, because the world of the book seemed so real. And besides, deep down, it was good to know I wouldn't really have to face Maugrim or the White Witch—because would I be as brave as Lucy? I didn't think I'd be as stupid as Edmund—I didn't think he could have read many fairy tales or else he'd have known the White Witch was up to no good—but I wasn't absolutely, *absolutely* sure. And I did love Turkish Delight. . . .

I identified with Lucy. Susan and Peter were a bit remote to me, like my bossy older sisters—five and seven years older than me, already in high school when I was still at primary school—

who stayed all the time in France in boarding school and never came to Australia with us, who we only ever saw when we were on our French holidays. Edmund was a bit like my younger brothers and sisters, who teased the dreamy, messy, storytelling girl I was, always trying to get them to act in plays I'd written or join me in "imagination games" I'd based on the books I read. Especially Narnia. From the first moment I picked up *The Lion, the Witch and the Wardrobe*, I loved Narnia. I loved everything about it: the landscapes, the castles, the magic, the adventures, the mouth-watering feasts. I especially loved the wonderful creatures: the Talking Beasts, the Fauns, the Centaurs, the Nymphs and Dryads, the Marsh-wiggles. I loved Aslan, but I also loved the villains—or I loved to hate them. They were scary, but they were powerful. You felt it really was something to fight against them. Narnia and its neighbors—Archenland, Calormen, and the Islands—were places I really, *really* wanted to visit. I wanted to know everything about them. I wanted to be there!

And I could escape there, any time I liked, in my imagination. C. S. Lewis made Narnia and its neighbors very, very real to me. I could see them, smell them, taste their food, hear their sounds, touch their trees, their stones, the fur of their Talking Beasts. . . . It was all just as real to me as the world around me. As real as Earth, the place variously called, in the books, Shadowlands, Ward Robe, and Spare Oom; the place of railways and timetables, school bullies and homework, family quarrels and rules; the ordinary, everyday, humdrum world familiar to legions of schoolchildren, where nothing much ever happens, where adults rule everything and you have no power and have to put up with all kinds of annoyances; where there's no magic or Talking Beasts, but there's always the threat of boredom. Narnia was never boring. There was always something happening. It was an enchanted world, bursting with possibility. Escaping to Narnia was wonderful.

So I devoured the first six books, my top favorites being *The Lion, the Witch and the Wardrobe*, *The Horse and His Boy* (I loved the Arabian Nights stories and this felt like that), and *The Silver Chair* (it was like traditional fairy tales I loved, and also reminded me of another beloved book, George MacDonald's *The Princess and the Goblin*). But *The Last Battle* was quite another story.

Oh, how I was disappointed by that book! It didn't feel like the other Narnia books, I thought. There was something wrong with it. And for me as a child the main thing wrong was that, in it, Narnia was destroyed. I did not want Narnia to end. I had no interest in that other world, Aslan's country, or whatever it was. I'd only half paid attention when it was mentioned in the other books. I didn't know about it, and I didn't really care. I wanted Narnia! Its loss made me very sad, sadder even than knowing that Lucy and Edmund and Peter and their parents had all been killed and poor Susan had been left behind to mourn and live on as best she could in "Shadowlands."

I was angry with Aslan, and puzzled. Why had he destroyed Narnia? Surely not just because of that silly business with Puzzle the Donkey and Shift the Ape? It felt like Aslan was punishing everyone in Narnia for no good reason. I didn't much like Prince Tirian, either. I thought he was a bit of a bore—not like Caspian, for instance. The book was much more serious than the others. There was no feasting to speak of. And when Narnia was finished, what did we get? Aslan's country! Big deal! You hardly knew anything about that place. It didn't live for me the way Narnia did. It didn't breathe. I closed the book rebelliously, thinking, "Well, I don't care! I'm going to pretend Narnia still exists! I'm going to pretend this book doesn't exist!" And so I read and re-read the other books, but left *The Last Battle* alone for years.

My parents are Catholics, and very devout ones, too. We were brought up with a very strong grounding in our religion at home and at school, at least when we were in Australia, which was most of the time (I went to a Catholic school in Sydney, but in Empeaux the village school was a state one and totally secular). I knew the Bible well, and the stories of the saints and I grew up with the symbols and images of Christianity deeply embedded in my soul. But still I had *no* idea that the Narnia chronicles had anything specifically Christian about them. Nobody told me they did. My parents did not read English-language children's books (though they read English-language adult fiction and non-fiction) and left me pretty much to my own devices as far as my fiction reading was concerned. Nobody at school told me either, because I didn't ask them. I didn't associate Aslan with Christ, and I only vaguely associated *The Last Battle* with Revelations, the last chapter in the New Testament—and that was only because they were both about worlds ending. Revelations was the part of the Bible I most disliked, anyway. I also vaguely associated *The Last Battle* with Ragnarok, or the end of the gods in the Norse myths—the part of *those* myths I most disliked.

I'm glad nobody told me back then. I might not have enjoyed the books as much as I did. Though I believed in God and had no quarrel with my religion, I preferred fairy tales, fantasy, and adventure to holy-type stories. Besides, to think of Aslan as Jesus back then would somehow have been embarrassing to me. And then where was Mother Mary, who was very important to us Catholics, too? The kind of ideas we were given about Heaven made it sound rather dull compared to Earth and certainly compared to Narnia. What child would want to just spend time mooching about a garden or playing on a harp or whatever? (We were once asked in scripture class to describe our own ideas of Heaven, and though most of the class dutifully described a garden or a beautiful country, one boy said he thought Heaven was a candy shop that never closed, where there was every kind of candy, you never had to pay for it, and you'd never get sick. Our teacher was horrified by the thought, but we kids thought it not a bad notion!)

It wasn't until I'd grown up that I realized Lewis was deeply Christian, and that this had partly inspired his writing of the Chronicles—at least, the part of him that analyzed what he was doing, not so much the storyteller. As he puts it in his interesting essay, "Sometimes Fairy Stories May Say Best What's to Be Said," the Chronicles first came to him the form of images: a Faun carrying an umbrella, a queen on a sledge, a magnificent Lion. It was only later that he realized this fantasy, this long fairy tale, might have a Christian underlay. This is what he says:

> I thought I saw how stories of this kind could steal past a certain inhibition which had paralysed much of my own religion in childhood. Why did one find it so hard to feel as one was told one ought to feel about God or about the sufferings of Christ? I thought the chief reason was that one was told one ought to. An obligation to feel can freeze feelings. And reverence itself did harm. The whole subject was associated with lowered voices; almost as if it were something medical.

Now, in my family religion is *not* associated with lowered voices. We are not a family—or a culture—that speaks with lowered voices! In fact, there were many lively discussions around the family table on all sorts of things to do with God and religion. But apart from the lowered voices bit, I could understand at once what C. S. Lewis meant. Though we might discuss religious things with great liveliness—we were not, as in the French saying, *grenouilles de benitier* (literally "frogs who live in holy water fonts," or holy Joes, if you like)—the central stories of our faith were approached with great reverence. Jesus was not a figure to regard lightly. He certainly didn't come from the same world as fairy tales. He was too big and important and serious. Nowhere in the New Testament is he shown laughing, and yet Aslan laughs a good deal. Holy stories, whether the Bible or the stories of the saints, don't have much time for fun, for feasting, and certainly not for magic. They have no light touch. There can be adventure and grand events, but you don't feel like you can take part in it, even in imagination. Everything is serious. Lewis was right. The stories themselves are power-ful, but the way they're taught, presented, shown to us, can be off-putting. Surrounding these stories is too often an *obligation* to feel. A feeling that one is almost trapped, listening to impor-tant stories, stories with a message you might be forced to learn by heart. Not in Narnia. In Narnia things were free, fun, magi-cal. Nobody preached to you or tried to force messages on you. At least it didn't seem so, until *The Last Battle*.

C. S. Lewis goes on to say in that essay:

> But supposing that by casting all these things into
> an imaginary world, stripping them of their stained-
> glass and Sunday-school associations, one could

make them for the first time appear in their real
potency? Could one not steal past those watchful
dragons? I thought one could.

Now that I was grown up and reading the Narnia books again,
for myself and to my own children, I could see the Christian
associations I'd missed. But I didn't say anything to my own kids
about it, at least not till they were teenagers. They too didn't
"get" that part of it, and it was only when they were told. But
like me, they too had instinctively disliked *The Last Battle*. So
did many other readers of the Chronicles, I discovered, though
by no means all. And then I began to wonder about the core of
the book, not only about the fact that it's the most overtly "religious" one, where the message tends to overwhelm the story,
the one based on Revelations (which remains my least favorite
part of the Bible), but also about Lewis's own feelings regarding
Aslan's country—or Heaven, as I now saw it was meant to have
been. What did he really feel about it, at least as a storyteller?
And so I started to look back through the books to find out.

We catch glimpses of Aslan's country several times in the
series. In *The Magician's Nephew*, Digory is sent by Aslan to a
beautiful garden on top of a hill by a blue lake in a green val-
ley. In this garden—based of course on the Garden of Eden—
grows the tree of life, with its lovely silver apples. One of the
apples Digory plucks is planted by Aslan and becomes the magical Tree of Protection for Narnia; the core of the other, which
brings Digory's dying mother back to life, grows into a tree on
Earth, where the wood is later used to make the Wardrobe.

The Garden also appears in *The Last Battle*, where it is
described fully and appears to be the world at the very heart of
all the worlds, the central part of even Aslan's country.

We catch another glimpse of Aslan's country at the end of *The Voyage of the Dawn Treader*, when Reepicheep leaves the others at the end of the furthest ocean at the furthest edge of the world. Just for a moment the children see a range of very high green mountains, and forests and waterfalls: a world that looks more beautiful and more real than anything they've ever seen. In several of the other Chronicles we are also told Aslan's country is "more real" than any of the other places we have been: it is richer, deeper, fuller, more colorful, with more meaning and wonder than any world we have seen or imagined. In *The Last Battle* we also see that Aslan's country not only contains all the other worlds he made, but the real, original versions of those worlds, not just the copy we have seen before now. Narnia still exists, then, in some strange way, even after Aslan has destroyed its supposed "copy" where so many wonderful and exciting adventures have happened.

But then Lewis tells us that looking at Aslan's country— or Heaven—after looking at the other worlds is like being in a room where you have a window on one side looking out to a landscape and a mirror on the other reflecting that landscape, and that Aslan's country is like that landscape in the mirror, not the one out of the window. I hadn't remembered that, and when I found it, and re-read it, I was puzzled. Surely a mirror world is *less* real than the one seen through a window! What is the point then of a new Narnia that seems less real to us than the old one? Lewis clearly intends for this to be part of the mystery of Aslan's country, where we see and hear with different eyes and ears and understand with different minds, and become young again. He tries to make Aslan's country seem exciting. But rather than *showing* this, as he does with Narnia, he *tells* us: it never feels quite real. When he writes about Aslan's country, he gets stiff, awkward. You feel like he approaches it with that same freezing, embarrassing reverence he talks about in his essay. Faced with Aslan's country—with Heaven—he can't make it quite real the way he does with Narnia.

Lewis certainly does not describe his heaven very much, except at the end of *The Last Battle*. This is partly because generally "sons of Adam" and "daughters of Eve" may only go there after death. It is a place from which no traveler may ever return, with the sole exception of Digory, who was allowed one very quick flying visit to the Garden at the time of Narnia's creation. But then, Creation is a very special time and universal laws are not yet in place. And the story of Narnia's creation rings true—there is something grand and awe-inspiring and beautiful and mysterious about Aslan/God singing the world into being, something that strikes deep into the heart as a poetic truth.

But I think Lewis is not very interested in Aslan's country at heart. He keeps saying it's a wonderful place, but we don't get a real feel for *why*. We do not know *what* happens there, if anything does. It is a place of refuge and peace and love and healing and wisdom, a safe haven after the toils and dangers of both Shadowlands and Narnia. There is no evil there—no struggle, no pain, no suffering, no conflict. This is all good, yes. But—and here's the rub—without those things there can also be no adventure, no search, no quest for wisdom, no excitement. Maybe it's a function of our limited human nature, but in this there can be no story we can understand or relate to. In the Chronicles of Narnia, it just feels like such an anticlimax after all the excitement that's gone before. (Just as, in my opinion, Philip Pullman's His Dark Materials—the mirror image of the

Narnia chronicles—also ends with a disappointing anticlimax, because the "Republic of Heaven" seems so dull; it just doesn't come to life in the way the old world did.)

Even though Lewis tells us "all their life in this world and all their adventures in Narnia had only been the cover and the title page: now at last they were beginning Chapter One of the Great Story which no one on earth has read," he fails to make the reality of Heaven—of Aslan's country—and the possibilities there live for his readers. That's why *The Last Battle,* which is so focused on getting to Aslan's country and getting rid of Narnia, doesn't work like the other books, or only occasionally does, in flashes. What C. S. Lewis did make live, gloriously and richly, were Narnia, and Calormen, and Archenland, and the Islands: wonderful countries of the imagination, the world he loved above all, and the reason why "going to Narnia" has remained a favorite pastime for millions of young readers the world over.

⧫•⊰•✵•⊱•⧫

Born in Jakarta, Indonesia, of French parents, **Sophie Masson** came to Australia at the age of five and spent the rest of her childhood shuttling between France and Australia. She is the author of many novels for children, young adults, and adults, which have been published in many countries. Just out in the U.S. in August 2010 is her book *The Madman of Venice* (Delacorte Press, Random House Children's Books).

Comedian Bob Hope once quipped that he left England at the age of four when he discovered he could never be king. But the lesson of Narnia is that you (and even Bob) can become a king or queen of your own life. Let the insightful Elizabeth E. Wein be your guide. . . .

—◆•▷◆※◁•◆—

Prince to King

Caspian's First Voyage

ELIZABETH E. WEIN

O nce a king or queen in Narnia, always a king or queen." That's what Aslan tells the Pevensie children, Peter, Susan, Edmund, and Lucy, as they take the four thrones at Cair Paravel in their first Narnian adventure, *The Lion, the Witch and the Wardrobe.* If you count pages, no king in C. S. Lewis's Narnia books actually gets more airtime than Caspian X. He plays a starring role in two books, *Prince Caspian* and *The Voyage of the Dawn Treader,* but in fact he's also king of Narnia throughout *The Silver Chair.*

From the day Caspian is forced to run away because his uncle Miraz wants to kill him, Caspian is called "king" by his tutor, the half-Dwarf Doctor Cornelius. The rest of the book describes how Caspian manages to win his kingdom back from Miraz. So why is the book called *Prince Caspian* instead of *King Caspian*?

I think it's because *Prince Caspian* isn't about Caspian's successful rule as an adult. It's about his journey to adulthood and to kingship—in *Prince Caspian*, the two are the same. Lost and alone in the beautiful, bewildering thicket of the trackless Narnian forest, Caspian has to find his own way. He has to learn to think for himself, to believe in himself, and to be responsible for himself. Only then, when he has mastered these three things—awareness, faith, and responsibility—can he take the throne as a true king of Narnia.

Awareness

The first of these characteristics, awareness, leads to and reinforces the others. Awareness means knowing yourself and knowing the limits of your own strengths and weaknesses, but it also means being aware of what is right and true. Our inner mind and heart know the truth, whether or not we choose to act on it. For C. S. Lewis, accepting one's inner truth leads to adulthood and kingship.

In *Prince Caspian*, Caspian is faced with two main challenges: he must restore Narnia, bringing its creatures and its magic out of hiding, and he must become Narnia's king. Both tasks mean doing away with deceptions that hide the truth—in Narnia's case, the truth that magic, mythical creatures, and Talking Animals exist; and in Caspian's case, the truth that he is Narnia's rightful king. In both cases, Caspian's uncle King

Miraz is the source of the deception. Miraz has silenced all mention of Narnia's true nature, and he has also denied Caspian's
right to the throne by styling himself king in Caspian's place. To
defeat Miraz, Caspian must strip away these deceptions, so that
true awareness can reign freely. But first Caspian must himself
become aware.

Caspian is a questioning child from the start; he wants to
know more about Old Narnia, and though his eagerness results
in his nurse being sent away, it results positively in Doctor Cornelius being hired as his tutor. Caspian is also quiet and watchful. He does not appear to be treated cruelly under the care of
King Miraz and Queen Prunaprismia, but even as a child he is
observant enough to realize that his aunt dislikes him and that
the kingdom is unhappy because "the taxes were high and the
laws were stern and Miraz was a cruel man."

Despite this, Caspian doesn't know who he himself is. Until
Doctor Cornelius tells him, Caspian is unaware that he is Narnia's rightful king. Once he is aware of the truth, he chooses,
rightfully, to act on it. . . . Though his first act as king of Narnia is what amounts to running away from home. This is Caspian's first step toward becoming who he is meant to be (who
he already is, Lewis suggests): Caspian must know in his heart
that Doctor Cornelius is telling the truth about his identity (and
Miraz's plans to kill him), or he would not have the courage or
desire to leave the castle.

Caspian's dawning awareness of Old Narnia's existence follows a similar pattern. He learns about it in nursery tales, and
although Miraz tells him the tales aren't true, Caspian never
gives up hope. When he learns that Doctor Cornelius is half-
Dwarf, it is enough confirmation of what Caspian has always

believed to be true that he enters the Narnian forest in search of its magical inhabitants.

This leads directly to "the happiest times that Caspian had ever known." He meets the three Bulgy Bears, Talking Squirrels, and the Red Dwarfs, who immediately hail him as their king. He meets Centaurs and Fauns, and Reepicheep the Talking Mouse, whose bravery and loyalty are limitless. Though Caspian now sleeps beneath the stars and lives on a diet of well water, nuts, and wild fruit, "he had never enjoyed himself more." Living in tune with—with awareness of—Narnia's true nature and his own changes him for the better: "he began already to harden and his face wore a kinglier look."

Faith

Caspian's choice to leave the castle, the only home he's ever known, requires faith: faith in his tutor's words, faith in himself, and faith in what he knows inside himself to be true. Awareness alone is not enough to make Caspian king; he also has to have faith.

The Telmarines, Caspian's ancestors, are men—sons of Adam and daughters of Eve—and it is this bloodline that allows them to be kings and queens of Narnia. But to be a *true* king or queen of Narnia, blood is not enough; you must also believe in Narnia. The reader assumes that, though the Telmarine kings who preceded Caspian might have fought against, feared, and silenced the inhabitants of Old Narnia, they never doubted their reality. It is Miraz, the usurper, who scorns Old Narnia as a pack of nursery tales. Narnia's true kings do not doubt Narnia, or the Lion who created it. The Narnian kings believe.

Caspian, who is raised as a prince regardless of his uncle's ambitions, pays as much attention to his old nurse's bedtime stories of Narnia as to his royal education. His belief in these tales wins him the Old Narnians' loyalty and Aslan's blessing. Even before Caspian has full control of his subjects, even when he has to fight to win his kingdom, he *believes* in Narnia. From the start, he wants to believe his nurse. He believes Doctor Cornelius on the night he advises Caspian to run away. He believes in the good of the blowing of the Horn of Need. When Peter, Susan, Edmund, and Lucy finally appear, Caspian never doubts who they are. He may waver when it comes to making decisions, but he never wavers in his faith in Narnia. Aslan never has to put Caspian's belief to the test, as he does to just about everyone else in *Prince Caspian*—especially poor Lucy, who ends up with the nasty job of having to follow the Lion's lead when no one else can see him. But when Caspian first meets Aslan, the great Lion simply gives him a face-to-face greeting and makes him king.

Prince Caspian makes another important point about faith. In *The Last Battle*, Susan is cut off from Narnia forever because she denies her belief in Narnia—and you can see her betrayal foreshadowed even in *Prince Caspian*, when she refuses to support Lucy's insistence that she sees Aslan, and that he is telling the children to follow him through the forest. Later, when Susan admits to Lucy that she never doubted Lucy saw Aslan all along, Susan says, "I really believed it was him—he, I mean—yesterday. And I really believed it was him tonight, when you woke us up. I mean, deep down inside. Or I could have, if I'd let myself." Faith, we see here, is a choice. Susan's denial comes because she chooses not to have faith in what she knows, deep down, to be true. In contrast, Caspian and the other Pevensie children choose to believe.

Responsibility

Responsibility can come in two different forms. The first is when you accept responsibility for something outside yourself: for example, a job that needs doing, like leading a battle or taking care of another person. The other kind of responsibility involves accepting the results of your own deeds, thoughts, and plans—taking responsibility for your actions. Often the two kinds of responsibility work hand in hand: when you accept responsibility for leading a battle, you must also accept responsibility for your role in the battle's outcome, even if your army fails.

When he becomes king of Narnia, Caspian accepts both kinds of responsibility. He makes considerable mistakes in leading his army of Old Narnians at first; he doesn't know enough about them to manage his army effectively. His very diverse Beasts and creatures love him and would do anything for him, but he keeps giving the wrong jobs to the wrong people— he doesn't realize "that Giants are not at all clever" and so he assigns a key battle strategy to the Giant Wimbleweather, who then accidentally runs out at the wrong time and loses the battle. And Caspian rightfully blames himself, not his subjects, for his early mistakes in understanding them.

When a fight breaks out at council and the Dwarf Nikabrik is killed, Caspian shows he is able to accept even a more personal responsibility. The fight happens in the dark. Caspian may or may not have slain Nikabrik himself, and says, "I don't know which of us killed him. I'm glad of that." Caspian doesn't like to face the fact that he might have done it, but he does face up to it—he knows he did kill someone in the fight. Caspian also accepts responsibility for the circumstances that led to the fight and Nikabrik's death. He blames himself for Nikabrik's death regardless of who may have delivered the killing blow; after the fight in Aslan's How, he says, "If we had won quickly he might have become a good Dwarf in the days of peace."

Caspian also learns to delegate responsibility when others might serve better than he can. Though he wants to fight Miraz himself, he knows that since he has been wounded by the werewolf he doesn't have the strength—and so he makes the responsible decision to allow Peter to fight the decisive duel in his name. Caspian puts personal pride and anger aside, and makes the best decision for Narnia.

L'Etat, C'est Moi: The King Connects to the Land

In Narnia, you can hide or disguise or forget yourself, or you can be ignorant or imprisoned or enchanted, but you can't fundamentally change your own nature. The land of Narnia itself is the same: it can be under an enchantment, such as the White Witch's, or under foreign rule, such as Miraz's. But at heart it doesn't change. And as Caspian awakens to his own identity, his growing certainty of himself and his kingship is mirrored in Narnia's awakening.

The Narnian landscape is a living thing. In *The Magician's Nephew,* when Narnia's magical creatures are created, they all pop up out of the ground itself. The land responds to its inhabitants, and its inhabitants to the land. . . . And this is especially true, it seems, of its rulers.

Consider the Pevensie children, who are already once-and-always Narnian kings and queens in their own right. When they arrive back in Narnia, called by Caspian's blowing of the Horn of Need, they don't know where they are or what their mission will be. Their own familiar castle at Cair Paravel is so long ruined and overgrown that it is scarcely recognizable. But gradually they recognize the layout of the castle and arm themselves with their own gifts from Aslan. They guess they might have a heroic job to do, even if they don't know what it is. They remember their adult selves as kings and queens, and they quickly grow comfortable in these roles. Simply by arming themselves Peter and Edmund look and feel "more like Narnians and less like schoolchildren," and after being in Narnia for only a day Edmund is ready to duel with Trumpkin: ". . . the air of Narnia had been working upon him ever since they arrived on the island, and all his old battles came back to him, and his arms and fingers remembered their old skill."

In the beginning of *Prince Caspian,* before Caspian knows who he really is or what his destiny will be, Old Narnia is only remembered in bedtime stories. The Talking Animals and mythical creatures are in hiding; the Dryads and Naiads, the spirits of trees and water, are asleep. In order for Caspian to become king he has to win these beings' loyalty, and before he can do that they must all be found and in some cases woken. A great deal of the action in *Prince Caspian* simply describes the gathering and waking of Narnia's citizens.

The wintry Narnia that Lucy stumbles across when she goes through the wardrobe for the first time in *The Lion, the Witch and the Wardrobe* is enchanted by the White Witch, and its people are in hiding or else have been turned to stone. The Pevensie children have to help time start moving again, to allow spring to come and bring the frozen land back to life. In *Prince Caspian,* though, Narnia is not laid *waste.* It is not frozen and dead. But it *is* dormant. The Dryads have gone back to being trees. The Talking Animals and other magical creatures have all disappeared. The few who are still around, Dwarfs and half-Dwarfs, have to disguise themselves as humans for their own safety. The task in *Prince Caspian* is to *wake* Narnia rather than to bring it back to life.

Caspian and his kingdom seem very closely connected; his forces only succeed when the two are completely united. His battle against the Telmarine usurpers is not won until the Old Narnian army of trees roused by Aslan and Bacchus joins forces with Caspian's army. Lewis highlights this connection by interspersing Caspian's adventures with the episodes illustrating Narnia's awakening. While Caspian is busy throwing off his personal enemies—the hag, the werewolf, Nikabrik, Miraz—Old Narnia is throwing off *its* enemies—the bridge that "chains" the river at the Ford of Beruna, nasty teachers, and mean-spirited children. Schools are closed, drudges are freed, the sick are made well. And Caspian becomes king.

"Once a King or Queen in Narnia, Always a King or Queen"

In *The Lion, the Witch and the Wardrobe,* the four empty thrones in Cair Paravel represent the Pevensie children's right to rule Narnia. But none of them can claim that right until all battles are won, justice is done, and order restored. Peter, Susan, Edmund, and Lucy are kings and queens by destiny and prophecy, but they cannot take those thrones until they have proven themselves, not just as heroes, but as individuals.

Caspian's flight from home, his first fumbling attempts at leadership, his councils gone awry and his missed opportunity to battle Miraz in single combat, all contribute to the experiences that ultimately make him a just and able king. He may have become a king as a child, but he has first proved himself capable of adult behavior. Once he has recognized his inner flaws and rejected them for his inner strengths, he becomes not just a king but an adult. For Caspian the journey to royalty and adulthood are the same: both journeys are about him finding out who he is. But Lewis tells us something else here. He tells us that the same is true for all of us. Once we know who we are, we each become a kind of king or queen in our own right.

In the Narnian view, if you are noble-minded, you don't need to be of noble birth or raised in a noble household. You don't have to have royal blood. You don't even have to be educated. You just have to have the strength to make your own decisions, to stand up for what you believe is right, to be fair and brave, and to be willing to accept responsibility and to admit to your mistakes. Regardless of their birth, the Pevensies are considered Narnia's greatest kings and queens ever, and their reign is called Narnia's "golden age." Their right to the four thrones in Cair Paravel is based on their having earned it through their own kingly and queenly actions. They are sons of Adam and daughters of Eve, and they carry their nobility through that unbreakable bloodline.

Any one of us could do the same.

Elizabeth Wein's young adult novels include *The Winter Prince*, *A Coalition of Lions*, and *The Sunbird*, all set in Arthurian Britain and sixth century Ethiopia. The cycle continues in *The Mark of Solomon* (Viking), published in two parts as *The Lion Hunter* (2007) and *The Empty Kingdom* (2008). Recent short fiction appears in Sharyn November's *Firebirds Soaring* (Firebird 2009). She's now taken off in a different direction with the forthcoming *Code Name Verity*, a thriller set during World War II. Elizabeth has a PhD in Folklore from the University of Pennsylvania. She and her husband share a passion for maps and flying small planes. They live in Scotland with their two children. Elizabeth's website is www.elizabethwein.com, and she keeps an erratic blog at http://eegatland.livejournal.com.

Ever notice how much effort the government puts into frightening you silly these days? Hardly a week goes by without some new warning about terrorism . . . global warming . . . bird flu . . . asteroid impacts. . . . But scare stories have been out there for a long time, and Susan Juby is about to tell you how, amid the doom and gloom, she found a ray of hope in Narnia.

—◆·▷·※·◁·◆—

Waking Up the Trees

Susan Juby

The animal shall not be measured by man. In a world older and more complete than ours, they move finished and complete, gifted with extensions of the senses we have lost or never attained.
—Henry Beston

The just man rages in the wilds
Where lions roam
—William Blake

The way I read him, C. S. Lewis was a tree-hugger. He was a don at Oxford and very dignified, so he probably skipped the tie-dye and the patchouli incense, but his Chronicles of Narnia, and especially *Prince Caspian*, suggest that he was as green as any modern day eco-freak. *Prince Caspian* can be seen as the fantasy equivalent of Al Gore's *An Inconvenient Truth*: it shows us that we human beings can become more responsible citizens of the planet Earth, if only we face the facts about the effects we have on our environment and let ourselves get a little closer to Nature.

Like many people these days, I'm concerned about the impact humans are having on the planet. Every day brings some new warning about global warming or other effects of pollution caused by over-development. But my concern isn't new. When I was nine, I was already on the lookout for litter-bugs and was an avid consumer of *Owl Magazine* and *National Geographic*. My favorite TV shows were Lorne Greene's *New Wilderness* and David Suzuki's *The Nature of Things*. I was fascinated with the magnificent variety of life on earth, but was also aware of how many creatures were becoming extinct because of human activity. As a result of my reading and learning about Nature and wildlife, I started to feel sort of bad about being human.

The books we read in school didn't help. Most of the better ones were quite depressing, pointing out all sorts of terrible dangers due to uncontrolled technology, environmental abuse, and corrupt government. *Nineteen Eighty Four* made me nervous of overhead cameras, *The Chrysalids* paralyzed me with fear of nuclear mutants, and *Animal Farm* created in me a phobia of repressive governments as well as Doberman pinschers. There was little in any of these books that offered much consolation, let alone hope. Perhaps that's why I treasure C. S. Lewis's Chronicles of Narnia even more today than I did when I first read them. Lewis, like Al Gore, points out the dangers of ignorance and exploitation, but he also holds out the possibility that we humans might yet change our ways and live and work in harmony with the rest of the natural world. It's a message we need now, more than ever.

In *Prince Caspian*, the fourth Narnian Chronicle, the Pevensie children—Susan, Peter, Lucy, and Edmund—find themselves pulled back into Narnia, where in the few months they've been back in Britain, several hundred years have passed. During this time, the real Narnia has been driven into hiding. The current king is a short-sighted, power-hungry man named Miraz, who has taken over the throne of Narnia by treachery. The one bit of hope is that the legitimate heir to the throne, the young Prince Caspian, longs for the old days, when "animals could talk, and there were nice people who lived in the streams and the trees." In fact, the first words we hear Caspian utter confirm his kinship with this earlier world: "I wish—I wish—I wish I could have lived in the Old Days."

What was old Narnia like? It was an environmentalist's version of heaven—an unspoiled natural place filled with abundant foliage and animals and birds. It was an uncorrupted land, in which the free will of its citizens hummed along in tune with the laws of Nature. It was like the Garden of Eden. (In fact, the Pevensie children are frequently referred to as the children of Adam and Eve.) Most important, Narnia was a land in which human beings lived happily and peacefully with the natural world. Like I said, heaven.

The Pevensie children find this former paradise in ruin. The wood is "so thick and tangled that they could hardly see into it at all; and nothing in it moved—not a bird, not even an insect." Only after considerable investigation do the children realize that they've landed at Cair Paravel, the seat of their former kingdom. In the years that they've been gone, Cair Paravel has become overgrown and intentionally isolated from the mainland by Miraz's people. Many of the animals are gone or in hiding. The trees, too, have slipped into a stupor: "Since the Humans came into the land, felling forests and defiling streams, the Dryads and Naiads have sunk into a deep sleep. Who knows if they will ever wake again?"

Not surprisingly, the people in this new Narnia have grown fearful of the Nature they've helped to destroy and from which they've cut themselves off in every way. In fact, the ruling Telmarines are "horribly afraid of the woods" and "in deadly fear of the sea because they can never quite forget that in all the stories Aslan," who represents the ultimate power in Nature, "comes from over the sea." Divided from the land, Narnia is "an unhappy country" because, as his tutor, Doctor Cornelius, tells Prince Caspian, the people have forgotten that Narnia is

> not the land of Men. It is the country of Aslan, the country of the Waking Trees and Visible Naiads, of Fauns and Satyrs, of Dwarfs and Giants, of the gods and the Centaurs, of Talking Beasts. . . . It is you Telmarines who silenced the beasts and the trees and the fountains, and who killed and drove away the Dwarfs and Fauns, and are now trying to cover up even the memory of them.

This destruction and the attempts to eradicate the memory of what was has left animals, humans, and the landscape impoverished and incomplete.

Today it feels like we've done the same thing in our world. Most of us, particularly those of us in developed countries, are divorced from the earth that sustains us. We live in our houses, shop in our malls, and drive in our cars. From fear and greed, we continue to exploit the wild places and wild things. Few of us have slept under the stars or even have any direct connection with the food we eat. In the twenty-first century, we are more separated from Nature than any Telmarine. And like the Telmarines, the less we know about Nature, the more we fear her. This is especially true now that our activities have begun to change the planet's climate and Nature seems to be wreaking revenge with powerful storms and harsh, unpredictable weather.

Yet, even a degraded Narnia pulls deeply, literally pulling the children out of the train station in England. Haven't we all experienced a similar pull? Don't we all desire, sometimes, to walk among the trees or watch the birds? Aren't we all called to witness the beauty and courage in even a spindly tree trying to survive on a busy street? The pull of Nature explains why parks are so crowded on beautiful days. It's not as though people flock to parking garages or newly cleared building lots! And this power of Nature's pull is felt everywhere throughout the Chronicles. Prince Caspian finds himself unaccountably drawn to those, such as his nurse and tutor, who are connected in some way to unspoiled Narnia (it turns out that both his nurse and his tutor are part Dwarf). The magnetic attraction of the natural universe is most emphatically symbolized by the conjunction of Tarva, the Lord of Victory, and Alambil, the Lady of Peace, which Caspian and his tutor witness from the rooftop. The two noble planets pass within one hundred degrees of each other. "Such a conjunction has not occurred for two hundred years," says Doctor Cornelius, and the event clearly signals "some great good for the sad realm of Narnia." Indeed, Prince Caspian's chief task in the book will be to discover how to bring the dormant creatures of Old Narnia back to life.

C. S. Lewis, like Al Gore, is a believer in the importance of "truth" as it pertains to man's relationship to the natural world. Thus, Caspian must confront his own divided attitude toward

Nature. After his escape from the castle, night falls and Caspian finds himself in a vast forest, where he remembers that he is, "after all, a Telmarine, one of the race who cut down trees wherever they could and were at war with all wild things." This inconvenient truth holds him in thrall, until Nature herself intervenes to save him. A storm whips up and his horse throws him, and he knows no more until he awakens to find himself in the care of a Dwarf and a Talking Badger. Caspian's education in the ways of Old Narnia has begun, and so begin the "happiest times that Caspian had ever known." In order to regain his connection to Nature, Caspian has to learn to understand her ways and to live in closer harmony with her creatures.

Before humankind can heal its relationship with the natural world, it must learn to trust in Nature, represented in the story by Aslan. Aslan shows himself first to Lucy, the youngest of the Pevensie children and the closest to Nature, who because of her innocence is able to see him. She trusts him completely. When he asks her to follow him, she tries to convince her older brothers and sisters to comply, but they refuse. They can't see Aslan, and they don't believe that Lucy can, either. When, as a consequence of their disbelief, the children hit a hopeless dead-end and have to backtrack, Lucy is again summoned by Aslan, who explains that she must gather her courage and this time convince her brothers and sisters to follow her, even if they must do so blindly. She is naturally frightened, for it "is a terrible thing to have to wake four people, all older than yourself and all very tired, for the purpose of telling them something they probably won't believe and making them do something they certainly won't like."

Such is the position in which many young environmental activists find themselves—trying to convince older family members that we must all change course if we are to avoid environmental disasters like global warming—but in one way, we are all like Lucy: we must all summon our courage and stand by our convictions until others come to understand their errors and are willing to change their ways. Eventually, through Lucy's commitment, the older children all eventually see Aslan as well. As Susan admits, she knew all along that Aslan was near: "I really believed it was him . . . I mean deep down inside. Or I could have, if I'd let myself. But I just wanted to get out of the woods. . . ." We can all sympathize with Susan. We know that we should pay more attention to Nature and face the inconvenient truth about the consequences of our actions, but it can be tempting to ignore our collective conscience because we are afraid.

We must reconnect with Nature in order to save it, but this involves overcoming fear and hardship. When Caspian first leaves the castle he is excited, but when the sun comes up "he looked about him and saw on every side unknown woods, wild heaths, and blue mountains, he thought how large and strange the world was and felt frightened and small." In working their way through the ecological disaster that has replaced their former paradise, the Pevensie children too experience fear, mostly fear that they no longer understand the land and the creatures they once knew. In one incident, the children shoot a grim gray bear that has been stalking them, and Susan worries that she might have killed "one of our kind of bears, a talking bear." Later, Lucy expresses her fear that someday men in her world might start going "wild inside, like the animals here" and it wouldn't be possible to know "which was which."

As frightening as the wilderness can be, frightening too is the prospect of losing the comforts of civilization; as Al Gore and other environmentalists suggest, to heal the earth we must learn to live with less. Caspian seems to thrive on the challenge:

> To sleep under the stars, to drink nothing but well water and to live chiefly on nuts and wild fruit, was a strange experience for Caspian after his bed with silken sheets in a tapestried chamber at the castle, with meals laid out on gold and silver dishes in the anteroom, and attendants ready at his call. But he had never enjoyed himself more. Never had sleep been more refreshing nor food tasted more savory, and he began already to harden and his face wore a kinglier look.

Likewise do the Pevensies thrive when faced with hardship. Their long walk through the woods heals the pain and stiffness in their bones, and the simple food—apples and wild bear meat—revives them. Indeed, after a period of hunger, the meal of bear meat and apples is described as "glorious." Even better, there is "no washing up—only lying back and watching the smoke from Trumpkin's pipe and stretching one's tired legs and chatting." I'm sure, of course, that not even Al Gore wants us to eat just nuts, berries, apples, and bear, but it's important to recognize that we could do just fine—perhaps even better—with a bit less of everything!

One of the lessons I take from Narnia is that the closer we get to Nature the more alive the world around us becomes. Lucy is especially attuned to this fact. She is the first one who hears the stirring of the trees as her siblings sleep: "A great longing for the old days when the trees could talk in Narnia came over her." She calls to the trees to awaken, but cannot bring them to life by herself; the others must also awaken to Aslan's presence before "all Narnia will be renewed." When Lucy summons her courage and convinces her brothers and sisters to follow Aslan, the entire land comes alive:

> Down below in the Great River, now at its coldest hour, the heads and shoulders of the nymphs, and the great weedy-bearded head of the river god, rose from the water. Beyond it, in every field and wood, the alert ears of rabbits rose from their holes, the sleepy heads of birds came out from under wings, owls hooted, vixens barked, hedgehogs grunted, the trees stirred.

A black mist appears to be moving toward them, and it turns out to be the reawakened trees "rushing towards Aslan." When we are ready to embrace Nature, Nature is always ready to receive us.

The most wonderful lesson in *Prince Caspian*, however, is that it is not too late to listen. As soon as the children begin to believe, Aslan forgives them and makes it clear what they must do. And when Caspian and the Pevensie children face down their fears and accept the truth, Nature triumphs and balance is restored. The reawakening of Old Narnia begins in earnest.

Some people see the planet and its non-human inhabitants as simply resources for us to plunder for our own benefit. Others (sometimes I'm one of these) see humans as sort of pests, seeking to devour the very Nature that supports them. C. S. Lewis, however, remained hopeful that, in understanding our weaknesses, we could learn to be responsible stewards of Nature. As Aslan, Nature's most powerful representative, tells Caspian, "You come of the Lord Adam and the Lady Eve. And that is both honor enough to erect the head of the poorest beggar, and shame enough to bow the shoulders of the greatest emperor on earth. Be content." Like C. S. Lewis, I would like to believe that humans have yet to play a vital role in the salvation of this heaven called Earth.

——◆◄►◆※◆►◄◆——

Susan Juby is the author of *Alice, I Think*; *Miss Smithers*; and *Alice MacLeod, Realist at Last*. All three books were bestsellers that were made into a television show called *Alice, I Think*. Her latest book is called *Another Kind of Cowboy*. She lives on Vancouver Island, B.C., with her husband James, their dog Frank, and Tango the horse.

You know how it is when you're a kid. No matter how sensible your opinions are, nobody listens. It seems to be a law of nature that the smaller you are, the less attention you're paid. But fortunately you have an important ally. When adults really get you down, tell them to go read C. S. Lewis. Susan Vaught explains. . . .

━━◄►◙◄►━━

It's the Little Things

SUSAN VAUGHT

Permit me to remind you that a very small size has been bestowed on us Mice, and if we did not guard our dignity, some (who weigh worth by inches) would allow themselves very unsuitable pleasantries at our expense.

Reepicheep the High Mouse offers these words to Aslan in *Prince Caspian.*

His meaning?

Stop picking on him and his fellow soldier-mice just because they're little guys. If you judge their worth by inches alone, you'll pay a wicked price.

As one of the fiercest and most influential warriors of Old Narnia—and okay, okay, one of the tiniest—Reepicheep knows that mice and children must always guard their dignity because older, bigger creatures use age and size as an excuse to dismiss the intelligence, skill, and usefulness of smaller creatures. Villains and heroes alike make that error all through the Chronicles of Narnia, especially in *Prince Caspian*, and it's—excuse the pun—a *big* mistake.

Too bad King Miraz didn't learn that lesson sooner. If the usurper king hadn't dismissed creatures smaller than him, he might have remained in power. Even worse, stars like Prince Caspian, High King Peter, and Lucy almost cost themselves their goals and their lives—and almost ruin Narnia's future—by doing the same thing.

All of these characters fail to grasp that smaller beings like children aren't weak simply because of their size. They aren't less worthy or less clever just because they're little or young, and they're definitely not less important in the battle for the soul of Narnia itself. In fact, in *Prince Caspian*, it's the children and the other smaller creatures of Narnia who decide the fate of the world.

As an old folk saying common to Narnia and the World of Men goes, *it's the little things that matter most.*

Dissing the Little Creatures

King Miraz proves himself a *big* fool when he makes his first and maybe his worst major blunder. He dismisses the little things of Old Narnia, namely the Dwarfs and intelligent Talking Animals. He tries to wipe them out, send them to sleep with the dinosaurs. He doesn't think Dwarfs and Talking Animals are important to the new Narnia, and he treats them like a mess he must tidy up before he can steal the throne from his nephew Prince Caspian. He's so focused on keeping these little things out of his way that he starts pretending Dwarfs and Talking Animals never existed, and he tries to convince everyone these creatures are just foolish myths and legends.

King Miraz even fires Prince Caspian's sweet old nurse for mentioning the older, more magical world of Narnia. This breaks Prince Caspian's heart and drives him away from his uncle. It makes the prince's mind and soul even more fertile for the fruits of King Miraz's next *big* mistake—failing to notice the significance of the strength and brilliance of Prince Caspian's new little tutor, Doctor Cornelius.

King Miraz hires Doctor Cornelius to teach the prince, but King Miraz never really looks at the doctor, never really attends to the truth of him or his hidden knowledge and power. King Miraz thinks Doctor Cornelius is no big deal, no big threat, just because he's little. King Miraz even sees Doctor Cornelius as "less than" because the small teacher doesn't look like he can hold his own in a physical battle.

Big mistake.

Even though Prince Caspian is "only a child," a lot younger than his uncle, it's Prince Caspian who first gets a clue about King Miraz's blunder in the case of the little tutor. Late one night on the great central tower of the castle, the truth comes to the prince in a rush:

> All at once Caspian realized the truth and felt that he ought to have realized it long before. Doctor Cornelius was so small and so fat, and had such a very long beard . . . He's not a real man, not a man at all, he's a Dwarf.

So, while King Miraz dismisses Doctor Cornelius as minor and without merit, while the king assumes that Doctor Cornelius is just another useless little thing, Prince Caspian sees the reality of his new tutor. It's Doctor Cornelius—the small, unassuming little Dwarf—who educates Prince Caspian. It's Doctor Cornelius who enlightens Prince Caspian in all the ways the prince so badly needs and craves, showing great courage in defying King Miraz's orders and in bringing Prince Caspian to a full understanding of his birthright and the untapped potential and plight of the barely surviving, carefully hidden citizens of Old Narnia.

Doctor Cornelius also possesses some bits and pieces of the magic of Old Narnia, and an appreciation for little things. He has spent many years and cast many spells to bring the prince the one (and surprise, surprise *small*) artifact of a bygone era that might be of use to Prince Caspian: the horn of Queen Susan, which the prince blows to summon the saviors of Narnia.

Finally, in an act of true and noble heroism, Doctor Cornelius puts his own safety at risk to spring Prince Caspian from King Miraz's castle. Because of Doctor Cornelius's bravery, Prince Caspian gets away clean from King Miraz and his forces before the king can murder him and obliterate the bloodline of the true kings of Narnia.

Prince Caspian then travels through the woods, into the heart of Narnia itself, and finds the Talking Animals, such as Trufflehunter the Badger. Trufflehunter is the first to swear allegiance to Prince Caspian as Narnia's true king, stating, "And as long as you will be true to Old Narnia you shall be *my* king, whatever they say."

Trufflehunter serves as a guide for Prince Caspian, leading him to other Talking Animals, such as Pattertwig the Squirrel, Reepicheep the High Mouse, Camillo the Hare, and Hogglestock the Hedgehog. Even though King Miraz doesn't think Talking Animals are worth much, these very small, seemingly insignificant creatures form the very army that follows Prince Caspian and rises up against the usurper king. Imagine King Miraz's surprise when he meets Prince Caspian on the battlefield, and the prince's army of Talking Animals holds off the royal forces.

Maybe the king should have paid more attention to those Animals he forced into hiding.

Even though he's a good guy, Prince Caspian himself starts off making the same mistakes as his uncle King Miraz. At first, Prince Caspian underestimates the smaller, weaker beings who have great influence on his life. His first potentially fatal excursion into his uncle's foolish oversights involves his own underestimation of Doctor Cornelius.

Prince Caspian goes to meet Doctor Cornelius on a deserted castle tower, alone, unprotected, and unarmed. When Prince Caspian really sees the true Doctor Cornelius for the first time, the prince thinks with a jolt, "He's a *Dwarf*, and he's brought me up here to kill me." Only Doctor Cornelius's pure intentions save the young prince that night. Had the small Dwarf been harboring ill or murderous intentions, no doubt Prince Caspian would have died before sunrise.

King Miraz's soldiers also exhibit this blatant disregard of anything smaller than themselves. Following King Miraz's lead, the soldiers underestimate a Dwarf they capture as he is on his way to search for the miracle the prince has summoned with the horn of Queen Susan. This Dwarf, ultimately known as Dear Little Friend (DLF), seems too small and weak to be a threat to the soldiers. As such, they dally and toy with him before finally losing him as a prisoner—a mistake that allows the return of Miraz's much more powerful enemies, the old kings and queens of legend.

One of those very same kings, High King Peter, makes a similar mistake. In the midst of the big battle with King Miraz's forces, he dismisses the worth and prowess of Reepicheep the High Mouse—and all his tiny warriors.

"Come back, Reepicheep, you little ass!" Peter shouts at Reepicheep and his soldiers when they join the fight. "You'll only be killed. This is no place for mice."

The Mice ignore him—and serve the greater good of Narnia.

But the Mice "[dance] in and out among the feet of both armies, jabbing with their swords. Many a Telmarine warrior that day felt his foot suddenly pierced as if by a dozen skewers. . . . If he fell, the mice finished him off; if he did not, someone else did."

At this point, Peter finally grasps the truth, as he doesn't make this error again.

As for Prince Caspian, after he escapes from his uncle's castle, the prince seems to finally *get* the lesson about appreciating the power of small things. He knocks off dissing the little creatures. In fact, by the time he starts meeting the creatures of Old Narnia, he accepts each being for its own gifts—or accepts that they have gifts, even if he can't see them readily as yet. He doesn't ridicule or dismiss the smaller warriors, but welcomes them all into his army. He also values the small horn of Queen Susan, and he uses it when Narnia's moment of desperation arrives. Maybe more important than all of that, Prince Caspian catches on to the serious danger associated with the dark Dwarf Nikabrik—the little freak who almost resurrects the evil White Witch in the prince's presence. Because Prince Caspian knows little creatures can be strong, he is able to recognize the evil Dwarf's threat. The prince saves his own life and the lives of many of his inner council.

So in doing so, Prince Caspian proves himself to be a hero who can learn, and perhaps a hero because he *does* learn, to accept the value of the smallest of creatures. He finds his way to an unlikely victory—a victory built on the little things.

Disregarding the Children

If anybody takes it in the dignity as much as tiny mice, it's children. Almost everybody in *Prince Caspian*, villain and hero alike, underestimates the kids.

King Miraz kicks it off by underestimating Prince Caspian. King Miraz treats the young boy as inconsequential and disposable. He assumes that no one so slight and young can stand up to him, much less wriggle out of his grasp. That's how King Miraz finds himself facing an army of Talking Animals led by this young, slight, and inconsequential child—who is in fact the land's rightful king.

The usurper king doesn't learn his lesson, though. Even after Prince Caspian surprises King Miraz, the king still screws up and decides that Edmund and Peter, because of their youth and size, cannot be the mythical kings from those nursery tales of grand Old Narnia. They are nothing but children, and therefore he sees them as no true threat to his safety. "Do you think I am asking you if I should be afraid to meet this Peter (if there is such a man)?" he asks his counsellors, who are exploiting this very prejudice to goad Miraz into accepting the challenge to single combat with Peter. "Do you think I fear him?"

In the battle itself, it isn't long before Miraz begins to feel the consequences of his error in judgment: "'Well done, Peter, oh, well done!' shouted Edmund as he saw Miraz reel back a whole pace and a half. . . . But then Miraz pulled himself together—

began to make real use of his height and weight." Thus, in this battle for his life, Miraz employs the same belief he had all along: that his superior size, his greater height and weight, will give him the advantage and bring home the fight in his favor. He thinks he's going to win simply because he's bigger and older, and therefore more experienced.

As the fight plunges onward, King Miraz gains the advantage over Peter, only to be thwarted at a crucial moment by the strength of Dwarf-wrought chainmail, which refuses to break under a death-blow. The craft of smaller, putatively weaker creatures proves to be the usurper's undoing. Before King Miraz can recover from Peter's next onslaught, King Miraz's own people murder him, and the usurper's story is forever finished.

If King Miraz hadn't assumed younger people were no threat to him, he might have been more alert. He might very well have stood victorious over all of Narnia, new and old.

Earlier in the story, Prince Caspian, for all his heroism, makes exactly this mistake when he fails to grasp the power and importance of his uncle's newly born son. The baby, after all, is only an infant, so tiny and helpless. When Doctor Cornelius insists that the child's birth places Prince Caspian in mortal peril, that the baby is responsible for King Miraz's change of heart and tactics toward Prince Caspian, the Prince responds with, "I don't see what that's got to do with it."

Doctor Cornelius has to remind Prince Caspian about the patterns of history, that when two heirs exist for the same throne, one heir almost always ends up dead. Prince Caspian now stands between King Miraz's son and the rule of Narnia; he's the "spare heir" and a potential usurper against King Miraz's blood-family. Thankfully, the prince understands before it's too late and runs away from his uncle.

High King Peter, in concert with Susan and Edmund, himself blunders in not trusting the smallest and youngest of his party, Lucy. Despite what occurred in *The Lion, the Witch and the Wardrobe*, when no one believed Lucy about her discovery of Narnia, and despite knowing that Lucy has a long history of truthfulness, insightfulness, and honesty, and that she is deeply connected to Aslan and the spirit-heart of Narnia, Peter still dismisses Lucy's claims of having seen the Lion. He also rejects Lucy's recommendations about how they should find their way to their destination.

When Lucy insists she has seen Aslan, Peter replies with, "Yes, Lu, but we don't, you see." Then, in making his decision to go against Lucy's pleas, Peter says, "I know Lucy may be right after all, but I can't help it. We must do one or the other." Peter chooses against her, effectively dismissing her perceptions, and leads his party to near-disaster. At least Peter is able to admit his mistake later, after everyone in his party almost gets killed—and after he realizes the truth of what Lucy told him, Peter finally sees Aslan again for himself.

Even poor Lucy underestimates a child—in a surprising way.

Lucy seems to have gotten so used to the belief that younger, smaller people are not as capable as older, larger ones that she fails to trust *herself*. When Aslan comes to her, and she knows with all certainty and absolutely no shade of doubt that Narnia's savior is at hand, she still doesn't have the faith in her own perceptions and strength to do what she needs to do. She lets her older siblings tap dance all over what she believes and doesn't stand up for her own assertions about the direction they need to take.

When Aslan confronts her later, she expresses her lack of faith by not believing he would have expected her to leave the others and follow him all on her own. Aslan gives her a look to let her know that, yes, that's exactly what he wanted her to do.

Lucy takes her lesson to heart, and in her next confrontation with her older brothers and older sister, she shows great courage and refuses to back down. She expresses her faith in herself and her own perceptions so strongly that they begin to believe with her. In turn, they rediscover their own ability to see Aslan, and they safely make their way out of the wilderness into the battle they need to join.

A Mighty Small and Large Lion

Contrary to the other inhabitants and visitors to Narnia, the Lion Aslan knows children and other tiny creatures have a power and strength all their own. He both seeks and counts on the smallest of creatures in all the land. He appears first to Lucy, the youngest of all, and offers her a fascinating paradox.

> "Aslan," said Lucy, "you're bigger."
> "That is because you are older, little one," answered he.
> "Not because you are?"
> "I am not. But every year you grow, you will find me bigger."

Thus, unlike everything else in life, Aslan gets bigger in perception as people age instead of smaller. He understands how children have been taught by society to see themselves as weak, how children are taught to be fearful. As a kindness, and because children are so important to him, he allows young people to see him at whatever size they can manage or accept. Aslan knows and respects the importance of little things so much that he specifically makes himself and all of his strength accessible to children in a powerful but non-threatening manner.

Aslan is also fierce with little creatures, children, and tiny animals. He doesn't let them off the hook when they don't achieve their own potential. When Lucy attempts to tell Aslan that her failure to win her siblings to her beliefs was not her fault, Aslan responds by looking her straight in the eye and letting her know he expects more of her, that she isn't excused from right action simply because she's small—or because what she's supposed to do is difficult. "It is hard for you, little one. . . . But things never happen the same way twice. It has been hard for us all in Narnia before now."

Aslan furthers his demonstration of respect for the little things by collecting the children of the village and treating them as important—even allowing them to ride on his back.

Additionally, unlike Peter and Caspian, Aslan fully blesses the efforts of Reepicheep and his Mouse warriors, granting them healing and honor. He reminds everyone that were it not for the tiny mice, his original victory against the White Witch would not have been possible, noting, "You ate away the cords that bound me on the Stone Table."

Aslan won't forget that kindness. He expresses the truth of his beliefs clearly in the statement, "Ah . . . You have conquered me. You have great hearts."

The Youngest, Smallest, Tiniest, Truest Truth

The littlest creatures and the youngest children are the real heroes of *Prince Caspian*. Though Peter, Edmund, Susan, and Caspian are knights and warriors who battle valiantly, they tap a courage they already know they have. They use abilities they know they possess and strength that, given their size and prowess, is no significant surprise. Essentially, these characters fulfill function and duty in a noble fashion. But heroes? Perhaps in form and function, but not so much with respect to heart.

For heroes in the truest sense, dig deeper into the pages and characters of *Prince Caspian* and understand that, yes, it's the little things. The bravest of characters in this tale are Doctor Cornelius and the Animals and Dwarfs who shelter and then join what appears to be a hopeless battle in support of Narnia's true King Caspian—especially Reepicheep the High Mouse and his warriors—and Lucy. They are the characters who face the overwhelming odds head-on, despite the failures and liabilities that make them doubt their ability to succeed. They throw themselves into the battle without hesitation or question.

Though young or small or in Lucy's case, both, they reach within themselves for a deeper, more powerful courage. They find strength that larger or older characters take for granted, and though they're frightened and outmatched, they battle anyway.

As noted by Aslan, these characters, these creatures and mice and children, are the genuine heroes who conquer with superior hearts instead of greater strength or weapons. It's the little things who rise, the little things who win the real war against society's dismissal and their own fears about their competence—and the little things who ultimately guard the world of Narnia with dignity.

———◆•▸▸•※•◂◂•◆———

Susan Vaught is the highly acclaimed author of *Exposed, Big Fat Manifesto, Trigger, Stormwitch,* and a number of books for adults. Her most recent releases include *Oathbreaker Part I: Assassin's Apprentice* and *Oathbreaker Part II: A Prince Among Killers,* an epic fantasy co-authored with her son JB Redmond. She is a practicing neuropsychologist and lives with her family in Kentucky.

As a youngster, Orla Melling was, by her own admission, "a scruffy, dishonest kid, living by the seat of her pants." She led a gang that let the air out of tires, threw stones through windows, and bullied other children. She was out of control, clearly headed straight for juvenile court. Then something magical happened. . . .

Being Good for Narnia and the Lion

O.R. Melling

W hich of your evil characters do you like the best?"

The question threw me for a loop, not the least because it was asked by a curly-haired girl-child, about eight years of age, with a face like a cherub's.

"Well, um, actually," I said, hemming and hawing to buy myself some time.

How could I answer without implying some kind of criticism or making the other kids laugh? I did a quick mental review of my published books at the time. Was Queen Maeve evil or simply acting the way a warrior queen should? What about the Tuatha De Danaan? They were a good race gone bad, but they do repent in the end and head off to be gods. As for Finvarra, the High King of Faerie, he was such a charmer even Gwen forgave him for the hard time he gave her.

"That's a very interesting question," I said finally, doing my best to be honest and careful. "I'm almost stumped. But, you know, I'm not big on evil characters and I'm not sure I really have any. I'll have to think about that some more."

Twenty years later, I am still thinking about the question and what it implied. Why are evil characters attractive? And should children's writers make evil characters attractive to their readers?

I'm not talking about attractive anti-heroes, like, for instance, Robin Hood. He may have been considered a criminal by the authorities, but we all know he was good at heart. Robbing the rich and feeding the poor, he was a hero who defied the evil rule of the Sheriff of Nottingham and his overlord, the bad King John. Luke Skywalker and the *Star Wars* rebels are a similar type. In both these cases, we can see quite clearly who's good and who's bad.

However, we begin to stray into the gray when we meet the handsome highwayman/bandit/pirate type, like Dick Turpin or Captain Jack Sparrow. Here we have robbers and even murderers who win their way into our hearts because they are good-looking and witty and roguish. We weep when they hang at Tyburn or cheer when they make their last-minute escapes.

Is it much of a step from liking that charming cut-throat to finding evil itself fascinating and attractive?

I recall a certain *Star Trek: Deep Space Nine* episode—you can catch episodes in reruns, if you're curious—in which our gallant crew ended up in an alternate universe where they encountered versions of themselves who were cruel, violent, and vicious. But also gorgeous. Was it one of the characters or a reviewer who commented on the confusion caused by discovering that your evil twin is hotter than you?

The world's most popular children's writer, J. K. Rowling, has expressed dismay at the number of her readers who claim Slytherin House as their spiritual home. Unlike many writers, Rowling has not made her evil characters attractive (though the movie-makers have, by casting good-looking actors for Draco and his father). Rowling's Slytherin characters are plainly liars, cheats, cowards, and bullies who will most likely grow up to be Dark Wizards who torture and kill men, women, and children. How could anyone find them attractive?!

Psychologists and others point out that young people often rebel against generally accepted opinion—Slytherin is bad, Gryffindor is good—and that this is normal and healthy. After all, Hogwarts is not real and Slytherins do have a Gothic counter-culture look about them, a hint of the fashionable vampire. I myself do not side with the do-gooders, moral majority fascists, and bootlickers on the side of "Right." There are many people, like Dolores Umbridge, who commit evil in the name of what is "good" and "right." Indeed, the meaning of these words—and what they are applied to—can get pretty muddled.

Enter: C. S. Lewis and the Chronicles of Narnia.

Big sigh of relief.

It cannot be overstated that, when it comes to C. S. Lewis, there is no question about what is right and what is wrong, what is good and what is bad. There is no marriage between heaven and hell, as the poet William Blake tried to argue, but rather "a great divorce," which is the name C. S. Lewis gave one of his

adult books written against Blake. And I, for one, thank him for
that. Why? Because, regardless of the gray areas in which adults
must play, this clarity made a great difference to me as a child
and to how I turned out.

Let me set the scene.

When I was five years of age, my family emigrated from Ireland to Toronto, Canada. After some moving about, we ended
up in a low-income housing estate with other displaced Euro-
peans—"economic refugees" we would be called nowadays—
from England, Scotland, Italy, Poland, and Hungary. All of us
felt deeply the loss of homeland, family networks, and small
rural or village communities where everyone knew each other.
Whether melting pot or mosaic, we were thrown into a stew of
foreign nationalities and urban anonymity. At the same time,
our families remained intact, and we all attended churches and
schools, practicing some form of Christianity. In my particular
neighborhood, all the children, both Catholic and Protestant,
attended a local, private community hall run by evangelists
where we got snacks, did arts and crafts, and had story- and
playtime. Along with the regular religious instruction we were
getting at home, school, and church, the evangelists' teaching
weighed in on the side of right and good with a colorful dollop
of hellfire and brimstone, sin and damnation.

And not one bit of it affected me, I can tell you.

You see, the 1950s was a dangerous time to be a kid. Cor-
poral punishment—a fancy word for assault on a child—was
rife. Any adult could hit you: parent, teacher, neighbor, clergy,
babysitter, shopkeeper, whoever. This widespread freedom to
cross a child's physical boundaries no doubt made it all the easier
for certain adults to cross sexual ones. Wherever physical abuse

of children is rampant, there too you will find sexual abuse. In short, as a kid, I struggled for survival in "enemy occupied territory," as C. S. Lewis called the world. In a time and place where children were "seen and not heard," trusting adults or believing anything they said was not a wise move.

So there I was, a tiny, skinny, undernourished little girl, with tangled hair and a dirty face, about seven years old, who wore slacks under her dresses (because you had to wear a skirt or dress if you were a girl in the 1950s, and this is how my sisters and I got around that rule). Founder of the Mischief Club, I led a small gang of girls and boys in such activities as letting air out of people's tires, throwing stones at windows, and ringing doorbells then running away, plus worse things such as tormenting small animals and bullying other children. I remember pushing a car—which we discovered by chance was not properly braked—down a hill and toward the main road. The driver came racing out of his house in time to catch it, even as we raced off, screeching with laughter. We didn't think about the possible consequences of our actions, that we could have caused a serious or even fatal accident.

Given the way I was going so young, I was possibly destined to follow some of the older kids into stealing cars, shoplifting, underage drinking, and whatnot (there were no drugs at the time, that I know of). Maybe. Maybe not. I'll never know, because something happened to stop my wayward decline.

Whatever else was going on inside and outside my home, there were always books, and I was always a reader. Though our family did not have enough money to buy books, my father made a point of bringing each of us to the library. I loved the library: the musty, woody smell of books; the shafts of dim light that fell through the windows; the hushed silence that mirrored my own awe. I started with Babar the Elephant and Madeleine and Rupert the Bear; but true reading didn't begin till one of my older sisters gave me *The Silver Chair.*

I didn't dabble in the Chronicles of Narnia, I drowned. A full-bodied baptism. There were many more books to follow, E. Nesbit's, P. L. Travers's, Patricia Lynch's, J. M. Barrie's, J. R. R. Tolkien's, and so on—but none had the same overwhelming affect. It was a conversion, short and simple. It started with an immediate love for Narnia itself. I suspect the beauty of that magical country touched upon the original loss of the green hills of Ireland and the blue waters of the Irish Sea.

But there was something more, something much deeper. The books slowly but surely changed me and my behavior. Someone once said that C. S. Lewis made goodness interesting. More than that, he made it *desirable.*

Firstly, his child characters were anything but prissy or sugary sweet. They bickered and fought amongst themselves, acted selfishly and thoughtlessly, were often greedy, jealous, cranky, and dishonest. They made mistakes, showed poor judgment, and failed in parts of their missions when they were tired, hungry, cold, or wet. In short, they were real, and just like me! Edmund's downward spiral in *The Lion, the Witch and the Wardrobe* was easy to understand. He was already in Peter's shadow, the Turkish Delight was delicious (spell or no), and the temptation of great power offered by an adult was simply too good to resist. Most of all, the way he lied to himself, convincing himself that he wasn't harming anyone and that the Witch wasn't bad, was so believable. I knew in my heart, *This could be me.* And even as I enjoyed how he suffered for his sins, slogging through the snow and being whipped by the Dwarf—*serves him right for what he did!*—I also felt the cold breath of justice that warned of the consequences of going wrong. For there was no doubt in my child's mind that Edmund's acts were evil, and that he knew what he was doing.

What a relief, then, to discover that Aslan's sacrifice could save the day, that redemption was possible. There was a ring of truth and rightness to it. Edmund repented and was forgiven and his change of heart made him a better person; indeed, more accessible than Peter, who seemed truly a High King and less fallible than the rest of us. In the later book, *The Horse and His Boy*, we discover that Edmund has grown to be "a graver and quieter man than Peter, and great in council and judgment," and this, too, made sense. I accepted that he had grown and matured from his experience.

Eustace Scrubb, on the other hand, in *The Voyage of the Dawn Treader*, was more fun to hate, as I didn't think he was like me. Still, I was won over by his change of personality, especially after the misery of being a dragon (eating the old dragon—a perfect moment!). By *The Silver Chair*, Eustace was a likeable and more sympathetic hero, though he still had his faults. Jill too displayed all the shortcomings of a real girl. Right from the beginning of the book, she caused disaster by showing off. And didn't Lucy herself, Aslan's darling, fall to temptation in *The Voyage of the Dawn Treader*? Only Aslan's interference stopped her from saying the spell of beauty that would have wreaked havoc on all around her (what girl could resist?). When stopped in that attempt, she quickly recited the one that allowed her to eavesdrop on a friend (again, who could resist?).

Even the Narnian heroes had bad sides! One of my favorite scenes was Prince Caspian's temper tantrum in *The Voyage of the Dawn Treader*. As a child, I was thoroughly impressed when he used his position as king to silence Drinian and demand his own way. Who would not be tempted to use their power that way? Then, of course, he was humble and sorry after Aslan visited him.

Like Shasta in *The Horse and His Boy*, I was a scruffy, dishonest kid living by the seat of my pants who was suddenly overwhelmed by the casual majesty and goodness of the Narnians. Like Shasta, I was instantly struck by Prince Corin's response to the suggestion that he must tell the truth to the others when they return: "'What else did you think I'd be telling them?' asked the Prince with a rather angry look." Here was someone with honesty bred into the bone. Again, like Shasta, I was surprised as well as admiring, because Corin was obviously no goody-two-shoes. One of my favorite characters, he was as mischievous as me and got into trouble on a regular basis. Yet he did not tell lies to keep himself out of trouble! He took responsibility for his choices and his actions! Later, in the tombs, Shasta reflected on his experience of meeting the Narnians in Tashbaan. "It was unpleasant to think of all those nice people imagining him a traitor." He cared what these good people thought of him.

And so, suddenly, did I.

Here were stories in which "being good" meant something entirely different than blind obedience and subservience to adult authority. In fact, being good often meant rebelling against cruel and unjust authorities. I couldn't help but notice that the good side in Narnia was usually the weaker side. In *The Lion, the Witch and the Wardrobe*, a small group led by children rose up against the White Witch and her totalitarian regime. In *Prince Caspian*, again it was a small group led by children who stood against the usurper Miraz and his army of adults. In *The Silver Chair*, we have two children and a Marsh-wiggle against the Green Witch and her hordes of enslaved gnomes. In *The Horse and His Boy* and *The Last Battle*, we have the smaller kingdom of Narnia threatened by the greater nation of Calormen. This underdog status of the side of right and good was an important point for a small and powerless child in a hostile world.

In fact, being good meant all kinds of things. It meant courage and compassion and honesty and justice. It meant adventure, high ideals, high-mindedness, heroic quests, noble causes, kindness to animals, and mercifulness to an opponent. To be good was to be noble: kingly, queenly, respected by and respectful of Talking Animals and the spirits of Nature. It also meant surprising things like humility: at the end of *Prince Caspian*, Aslan asked the young prince if he felt ready to take up the kingship of Narnia: "'I—I don't think I do, Sir,' said Caspian. 'I'm only a kid.'" Then Aslan stated quite plainly that only this answer gave him the right to be king.

Most of all, being good meant pleasing Aslan; being one of His own and beloved by Him. And oh, how I wanted to please Him, my first and only understanding of a loving God. For Him, I aspired to be good, not in the smaller sense of obeying rules and pleasing adults, but in the much grander sense of becoming a better person with high moral principles. Yes, that shabbily dressed, unkempt, underfed wild-child aspired to the Medieval virtue of "nobility."

And she knew full well it would not be an easy road. All the warnings were there in the books. Aslan expected your best.

Indeed, regardless of whether it was fair or not, he expected you to be better than the adults around you. In *Prince Caspian*, when Lucy, the youngest, was the only one who could see him and the others insisted on going a different way, still he expected her to follow him, no excuses! She could not use her youth or her fears or the others' bullying to let her off the hook. This was always quite clear in the Chronicles. Being a child did not excuse you from doing what was right. Children were continually called upon to be brave, to face hardship and difficulty, and to continue against all adversity to do what was right no matter the obstacles, no matter the consequences. Oh the power of it! Aslan's standard called to the king and queen inside every boy and girl. *For Narnia and the Lion!*

What child wouldn't be awed and perhaps a little frightened, but also proud and pleased, to realize that she is as free and responsible as any adult to make her own moral choices and to forge her own character from those choices?

There were no gray areas here. No slippery slopes. Aslan was a hard taskmaster, pure as light, sharp as steel. I distinctly remember being shocked and discomfited when he explained to Aravis, in *The Horse and His Boy*, that she had to suffer the same pain, lash for lash, as the slave girl she had drugged in order to run away from home. Like Aravis, I thought the slave girl's whipping was fair enough, given that she was a spy. But no, Aslan's justice was strict and pure. The razor's edge. No excuses. No gray areas. The slave girl suffered as a direct result of Aravis's actions and that put Aravis squarely in the wrong. I remember gulping at this even as I caught a glimpse of a moral code beyond anything I could have imagined with my child's sense of fairness. The bar was raised—to heaven.

And in the stories the truth was told again and again: the path of right and good would not be an easy one. In *The Horse and His Boy*, when Shasta goes back to help Aravis and Hwin, standing up to the lion despite his terror, the narrator tells us bluntly, "if you do one good deed your reward usually is to be set to do another and harder and better one." I remember liking this as a child. I appreciated the stark honesty. No sugar coating about the way I was thinking of going. And I also liked the challenge. The difficulty itself made it appealing: something of value, worth the effort. A pearl of great price. And there was always the promise, the stories showed that too, that when I inevitably fell or failed, I would not be abandoned, I would not be rejected. I would be forgiven and supported and ever part of the fold.

Truly, looking back, I see that the twists in that little girl's soul—warped by the evils of her environment, both church and society—were being hammered out, like a silver sword forged by the clarity and purity of C. S. Lewis's vision. And it was not done with force or fear, nor with fire and brimstone, but with love and magic. It was laid out before me, a shining path, and the decision was entirely up to me: Would I follow Aslan or not? Would I aspire to his sense of right and wrong? Would I choose good over bad?

There was nothing attractive about evil in the Narnian Chronicles. The bad side brought misery to everyone: the White Witch's eternal winter with no Christmas; Miraz's regime where animals were forbidden to talk and magical creatures had to hide; the gloomy desperation of the little gnomes in silent bondage to the Green Witch; the desolation of Charn where all life was eradicated, accompanied by Aslan's warning to Digory

Kirke and Polly Plummer that "great nations in your world will be ruled by tyrants who care no more for joy and justice and mercy than the Empress Jadis." Who would want to side with that?

Better was the hero's path that was also the way of joy: feasting in castles by the sea, dancing in woodlands under the moon, festivals and orchards, jewels and beautiful clothes, sweet-natured animals and enchanting creatures, kings and queens of noble manner.

At nine years of age, I chose the path of right and good under C. S. Lewis's guidance.

And here let me speak against two major criticisms aimed at this series. Firstly, the charge of racism. While Calormen, the literary foil of Narnia, is clearly inspired by Arab culture, one cannot ignore the fact that two beautiful characters hail from there: Aravis of *The Horse and His Boy*, future queen of Archenland, and Emeth, the gracious young Tarkaan in *The Last Battle*, cherished by Aslan. Notwithstanding the significance of these two, I truly believe that anyone who aspires to the high ideals of the Chronicles could *not* tolerate the evil of racism. I recall expressions of racism around me as a child, which I found offensive. When I could, I objected to them, even against adults. Where did I learn that racism was wrong? I can assure you it wasn't from television or home or school or church. None of these institutions in the 1950s spoke out against it. I do believe I learned it was wrong from C. S. Lewis. The core sense of goodness and decency that he inspired in me led me to recognize and reject this evil.

There is also the charge of sexism against C. S. Lewis. Given the time when he was writing, the roles he gave to his girl characters—so central and heroic—are astonishing. How can anyone not see that Lucy is the prime player and Aslan's favorite? Jill is such a Girl Scout, such a courageous adventuress, while Aravis is cultured, intelligent, independent, and opinionated, a true queen of a girl. As for Susan and her "nylons and lipstick," I always understood this to be the author's way of showing yet another moral choice: the worldliness of materialism versus the path of the soul. Narnia did not reject Susan, she rejected Narnia, and she was free to do so. We are all free to do so.

It has been said that C. S. Lewis wrote the Chronicles to instill in children a love of goodness and Aslan, which would grow in time to their acceptance of Christianity. Interestingly enough, the first happened to me but not the second. I loved Aslan and wanted to be good, but I did not embrace Christianity as I grew older. The Christianity I met in the real world never matched the goodness I met in Narnia; hence, I did not and still do not relate one to the other.

But ah, my dear beloved C. S. Lewis. I am so grateful to this author who rescued me from the nightmares of my childhood. Indeed, he set me on a spiritual path which has strengthened and supported me throughout my life. I have never forgotten the Chronicles, nor the song of the soul first sung to me by Aslan. I will always aspire to be better than the ordinary me who continually fails in that aspiration; for at a very young age I set my moral compass by Narnia and the North.

◆➤◗▓◖◄◆

O.R. Melling was born in Ireland, grew up in Canada with her seven sisters and two brothers, and now lives in Ireland again. She has published eight books, many of which have been translated into various languages. The four books of her Chronicles of Faerie (named in homage to C. S. Lewis) are *The Hunter's Moon,* *The Summer King,* *The Light-Bearer's Daughter,* and *The Book of Dreams,* published in America by Harry N. Abrams, Inc. Her new mythological adventure series, *The Celtic Princess,* will be published by Penguin Putnam in 2011. Melling lives in a small town by the Irish Sea with her daughter Findabhair and her cat Emma. Visit her website at www.ormelling.com.

The French writer Jean-Paul Sartre decided that to be was to do. The German philosopher Friedrich Nietzsche claimed that to do was to be. The American singer Frank Sinatra summed it up in the immortal words, Do-be do-be do. . . . The whole question of doing and being can be especially vital to a teenager, as Zu Vincent and Kiara Koenig have discovered. They ask the burning question, inspired by C. S. Lewis: Are you a Susan or a Lucy? Think hard before you answer.

◄►►◄►◄►

Mind the Gap
Are You a Susan or a Lucy?

ZU VINCENT AND KIARA KOENIG

O ne of the most delightful things about reading books is what they can tell us about ourselves. We live with a character and follow him or her through the story with our own fingers numbed by the cold they suffer and our eyes dazzled by the wonders they see. When it comes to the Pevensie girls in the Chronicles of Narnia, whom do you feel most drawn to, Susan or Lucy? The reasons for your answer might surprise you, since C. S. Lewis used these characters to explore the age-old dilemma: how to grow up without becoming "very" grown-up.

What does this mean? The answer lies in the difference between *being* and *doing*. That is, between being who you are and doing what others expect of someone your age.

Look at the four Pevensies. When they first enter Narnia, they're just kids. But by the end of the story they've matured enough to defeat the Witch and take their places as Kings and Queens of Narnia. They don't just appear grown-up by the end of the book, they've become better people, stronger and more emotionally mature.

Yet Lewis understood that gaining this emotional maturity isn't always easy. And in the Chronicles he used the two Pevensie girls, Lucy and Susan, to show this journey—a journey that centers on the struggle between acting grown-up and really growing up. A journey reflected in the act of reading itself.

◄ ►◄►◄※►◄►◄ ►

Do you find yourself tucking a fairy tale behind a copy of *Teen Vogue* to escape notice? Or hiding a novel under your backpack for fear someone will tease you because you're "still reading those books"?

We don't live in a reader-friendly world. There are few quiet corners in which to curl up and open a good book. Even fewer moments when we can just be alone and think. It's often easier to not think too deeply, to instead watch a movie, play a video game, or surf the net. And it's hard to hear the voices of stories, which are softer than the rustle of pages, over the ring tones of incoming text messages.

Or maybe you have someone nagging you to "get your nose out of that book" and *do* something. As if reading were something we needed to outgrow along with naps, stuffed animals, and imaginary friends.

But a story, unlike cell phone minutes, is never ending. Because they are more than the sum of their plot, stories don't lose their ability to make us laugh once we know the punch line or to spark our curiosity even after we know "whodunit." Like the best dessert in the world, the more you have, the more you want. But unlike the Witch's enchanted Turkish Delight, stories nourish us as we read.

They're gateways, and the further up and further in we go, the richer the tale, the realer the world, the more intense the experience. Stories ask us to come inside and do half the work of making them come alive if we want to feel their full magic. A magic that takes us deep into the core of what makes us human.

◆•⋙•✷•⋘•◆

Nowhere is this friendship with the reader more apparent than in the opening book of Lewis's Chronicles of Narnia. After all, *The Lion, the Witch and the Wardrobe* begins with the invitation: "I wrote this story for you. . . ." This invitation was originally meant for Lewis's goddaughter, Lucy Barfield. But all readers are welcome, as long as they venture through the wardrobe door with Lucy Pevensie's sense of curiosity and her willingness to engage with what's inside.

Think of Lucy's first encounter with the Faun, Mr. Tumnus. She's neither suspicious nor fearful. She greets him with a polite "Good evening," and they're soon walking together "as if they had known one another all their lives." Good stories have the power to take us by the arm and lead us into a world so real we believe in it totally. They help us see beyond differences like horns and furry legs to shared pleasures like tea and sardines. Which is why Lewis firmly believed fairy tales weren't just for children. To the author they were a way of better understanding ourselves. "When we read myths," wrote Lewis in his book of essays *On Stories*, "we do not retreat from reality: we rediscover it." But if this is true, why do so many people think fairy tales are just for kids?

Lewis believed that those who dismiss fairy tales do so because they can't see past the surface of the story. They get distracted by the fact that badgers can't talk and centaurs don't exist, and never learn to see the reality fairy tales expose. For Lewis, these are the readers who aren't really grown-up, but who are instead trying desperately to *appear* grown-up by acting as others expect.

But there is another type of person, another type of reader, who is mature enough to *be* grown-up and look beyond the surface to what actually matters. It is these two types of people that Susan and Lucy represent. Susan pretends to be "very" grown-up, but Lucy stays true to herself no matter her age.

Acting grown-up means worrying exclusively about the kinds of things Susan frets over in the Chronicles, such as bedtimes or what to wear to a party. Real maturity is simply living based on what you know to be right, living as who you are at your core, right now. Maturity allows Lucy to save Narnia, because it allows her to see the magic that makes Narnia unique.

The personality contrast between Susan and Lucy is apparent in the opening pages of *The Lion, the Witch and the Wardrobe*. The Narnian adventures begin when Lucy follows her curiosity, first by trying the wardrobe door, and then by venturing into Narnia and her tea date with Mr. Tumnus. Susan, in contrast, tries "to talk like Mother," as Edmund points out, sending the younger kids to bed and playing peacemaker in their squabbles. When she opens the wardrobe door, it's nothing but a wardrobe, plain and simple. For Susan, the world is what it appears to be.

Susan isn't a bad person. She's just trying to act like a grown-up.

Even though Susan isn't an adult, she feels it's her responsibility to behave as one in her mother's absence. She's trying very hard to do the right thing by keeping her younger siblings in line. Trying *too hard* is the point. Her idea of how adults should act is already shaped, and she wants desperately to be seen as one.

When the Professor suggests they accept that Lucy has in fact been to Narnia, Susan can hardly believe it. As Lewis writes, "She had never believed that a grown-up would talk like the Professor and didn't know what to think." In Susan's mind being an adult means being practical and responsible, and the Professor is being neither. When he answers her question, "But what are we to do?" by telling her to mind her own business, she decides that perhaps he's not quite right in the head.

There are benefits to Susan's practical nature: when all four Pevensies finally venture through the wardrobe and into the "always winter and never Christmas" landscape of the Lantern Waste, Susan suggests that they take some of the coats in the wardrobe to keep warm. As she logically points out, it's not as if they will even "take them out of the wardrobe."

Lewis doesn't want us to hate Susan. Through her, he wants us to understand the risks of relying on appearances and getting too comfortable with judging based on expectations.

These risks include an inability to see past the surface. Like many of us, Susan later falls for a pretty face, only to discover the monster underneath. In *The Horse and His Boy*, she's smitten with Prince Rabadash because he performed "marvelous feats" on the tourney field and "meekly and courteously" conducted himself during his visit to Cair Paravel.

Others are not so convinced. Edmund points out Rabadash's failings, telling Susan, "It was a wonder to me that ever you could find it in your heart to show him so much favor." In truth, Rabadash is both arrogant and deceitful, concerned only with his own greater glory. Even losing soundly on the battlefield can't teach him maturity.

The danger of relying on appearances becomes even more apparent if we compare Rabadash to Puddleglum (the Marshwiggle from *The Silver Chair*). At first glance Puddleglum doesn't seem like the heroic type. He's gangly and gray, not tall and handsome. He lives in a salt marsh wigwam, not a palace. He's always certain that the worst will happen, that they'll all be killed, eaten, or lost forever.

Yet unlike the dastardly Rabadash, he's brave in spite of his fears, not to mention loyal and resourceful. Puddleglum shows us that even in the worst of times, we can make things better by making new friends, going on new adventures, by believing that risking failure is better than not trying at all. But he's the kind of character someone concerned with appearances would overlook completely. He's certainly someone Susan would never fall for in a million trips to Narnia.

He's someone Lucy would take to in a heartbeat.

◆◆◆◆

Lucy's insight into the world around her is different than Susan's. We see this in *Prince Caspian* as the Pevensies struggle through the overgrown forest between Cair Paravel and the Stone Table. They argue over which path to take, and Lucy, certain she has seen Aslan, tries to convince the others to go upstream. Susan argues that going downstream makes more sense. She reasons that they can find their way from the river. Besides, she isn't at all convinced that Lucy has actually seen Aslan. She even implies that Lucy imagined him.

Susan is once again trying to be the practical grown-up. Her goal is to get out of the woods so they can join Caspian and defeat Miraz. Lucy isn't worried about escaping the woods. She's too busy wishing the trees would wake up. In fact, all of the Pevensies except Lucy are focused on finding the shortest route and on the logistics of defeating Miraz's army.

But Narnia cannot be kept alive by swords alone. We've already learned this lesson in *The Lion, the Witch and the Wardrobe* through Aslan's self-sacrifice and his thawing of the animals. As much as Peter's battlefield defeat of the Witch, these acts were necessary in order to restore Narnia and melt the ice of the Witch's winter forever.

In his stories, Lewis reminds us that while evil must be defeated, that is just the first step. Real healing means restoring what was lost. This is Lucy's role. She connects to Narnia in its truest version: the Narnia of the Nymphs and the Dryads, of the river god and Mermaids. More than Peter's sword fight with Miraz, it's Lucy's desire for Caspian's Narnia to reawaken to its own magic that restores the land to full glory.

But restoration comes at a price. Often, it means risking going it alone, following a path only you know is the right one. As Aslan tells Lucy, "Go and wake the others and tell them to follow. If they will not, then you at least must follow me alone." At that moment Narnia's fate lies in Lucy's ability to either convince her companions of the truth or move forward on her own.

◆•▷▪❋◁•◆

Those of us who have to defend our interest in fairy tales recognize Lucy's dilemma. How can we possibly convince those practical "grown-ups" that fairy tales are not childish, but as necessary as good food? How do we prove to them that we're not wasting our time in imaginary worlds, but instead discovering what makes life worth living?

And there's a danger for us here too. Will we lose our ability to see the truth, to be ourselves, when we're face to face with what others think? Naturally, as we grow up, we try new things and get wrapped up in friends, looks, and flirtations. But living by what others expect of us can lead to a false sense of maturity.

On the London underground they say to "mind the gap," to be wary of the space between the train and the station platform. While the gap on the underground is a physical hazard, we can stumble on spiritual hazards too. Like Lucy, each of us experiences stages in our life's journey when we're certain of who we are and the direction we need to go. Our goals are our own, and we move through the world with confidence and an open heart, we "mind the gap" and step over what threatens to trip us. But between these stages are those moments of change and fear when our inner wisdom fails and we risk becoming like Susan, who, even though she was once a Queen of Narnia, has fallen into this spiritual gap. She may act "older" but she's not necessarily wiser. Perhaps the most telling comment about her is Prince Corin's. In *The Horse and His Boy*, Corin tells his brother, "She's not like Lucy, you know. . . . Queen Susan is more like an ordinary grown up lady."

Trapped by her need to appear grown-up, she's lost sight of Narnia. "Fancy your still thinking of all those funny games we used to play when we were children," she says to her siblings when they try to keep their memories of Narnia alive in England.

In contrast, Lewis reminds us through Lucy that holding on to what you love isn't a game, and staying true to ourselves is at the heart of maturity. Remember in *The Voyage of the Dawn Treader* when Lucy reads the Magician's Book of Spells and almost succumbs? She's searching the book for the Monopods' visibility spell when she's lured by the incantation to make its reader beautiful "beyond the lot of mortals."

But as the book shows Lucy herself transformed, it also shows her the consequences. First she's adored, then her beauty causes full-scale war in Narnia. Even in the real world, her beauty makes her so important that "no one cared anything about Susan now." The spell tempts Lucy to become someone other than herself, someone everyone will notice.

Lucy wants to say the spell even knowing the evil it will cause. But Aslan helps her resist. As a result, Lucy reads further and finds "the spell to make hidden things visible." She says the spell and Aslan appears. To her surprise he reminds her that she herself has the power to make things happen, just as she is. "'I've been here all the time,' said he. 'But you have just made me visible.'"

<hr />

Lucy is able to stay true to herself throughout the Chronicles of Narnia. Susan has a different fate. In the final book, *The Last*

Battle, while Lucy still drinks "everything in more deeply than the others," Susan is "no longer a friend of Narnia."

When you're no longer a friend of Narnia, the Narnian adventures will seem silly and simple. You'll stop believing in Talking Animals and "living" trees, anything that doesn't appear in the grown-up world. And you'll forget that the important magic of Narnia is its ability to teach us about the good and evil in human nature. But even then, some small voice may remind you of what you once loved—the magic of possibility.

Perhaps you'll see this magic in the way fall leaves whirl themselves into miniature tornados of gold, cinnabar, and crimson, reminding you that even in the cold there is beauty. Or maybe you'll meet someone new who bounces from one moment to the next like a Monopod, as if their calves and their emotions were built on springs.

◆·)◑·※·◐(·◆

"The value of myth," Lewis argues in his review of Tolkien's *Lord of the Rings* in *On Stories*, is "that it takes all the things we know and restores to them the rich significance which has been hidden by the 'veil of familiarity.'"

To understand what he means, think of how good food tastes when you've been reading a tale in which the characters go hungry. Or of how much you appreciate your bed when the characters are sleeping on stone in the rain, huddled under damp, smelly wool cloaks. "By dipping [everyday things] in myth," Lewis says, "we see them more clearly."

To see clearly, story takes us back to a time when the whole world spoke to us. When the constellations were our palm readers and even the stones could warn us of the coming of our fate.

Today's science describes the stars as novas, supernovas, and galaxies, and locates them by their relative distance from our solar system. But this practical information brings us only so close to true understanding.

"In our world . . . a star is a huge ball of flaming gas," Eustace tells the "retired star" Ramandu in *The Voyage of the Dawn Treader*. Ramandu replies, "Even in your world, my son, that is not what a star is but only what it is made of."

Stories do not just describe the world, they teach us what it really is. And, like Lucy and Susan, what we're really made of.

◆·▸◆·※·◂·◆

In the end, the world is more than an objective description of its continents, weather patterns, and animal populations, just as each of us is more than our height, weight, and hair color. If we get distracted by the surface, we can forget this truth. Lucy learns this in the hallway of the Magician's house in *The Voyage of the Dawn Treader*—by getting a reminder that, often, what scares us is quite harmless.

When the "wicked little bearded face" jumps out and scowls at her, she "force[s] herself to stop and look at it." Because she makes herself really look, she discovers it's "just a little mirror . . . with hair on the top of it and a beard hanging down from it." Though the hair and beard fit as if they were part of her, she's able to see the illusion for what it is and continue her journey.

It's like Halloween. Once you recognize who's under the costume it's not scary at all. At the same time, the mirror is a warning. If we let ourselves become someone we're not, if we let others choose how we dress and act and what we believe, then one day we'll look in the mirror and hate our own face.

So the next time someone tells you to put down that book, remind him that, as Lewis points out, it's our own humanity we rediscover, our tendency toward "good and evil, our endless perils, our anguish, and our joys." Stories are mirrors that show us our soul.

If the Chronicles of Narnia convince us of nothing else, they should convince us that we do not have to give up what we love. "No book is really worth reading at the age of ten," Lewis reminds his readers in *On Stories*, "which is not equally (and often far more) worth reading at the age of fifty." Books worth savoring at any age are those that open doorways into other worlds, each of which is more real and more beautiful than the last, and such books open doorways within us as well.

"When I became a man," Lewis writes, also in *On Stories*, "I put away childish things, including the fear of childishness and the desire to be very grown up." If we stay true to ourselves, then we'll be rewarded. In *Prince Caspian* Lucy wakes her siblings and insists they walk upstream. Even when Susan threatens to stay behind, Lucy doesn't cave in. She does what her heart tells her and trusts her vision of Aslan and her love of Narnia to lead her in the right direction.

Once the others follow her, their trust in Lucy allows them to see Aslan too. When Susan finally sees him, she tells Lucy, "I really believed it was him. . . . I mean deep down inside. Or I could have if I'd let myself."

This gives us hope that the woman Susan has "grown into" by *The Last Battle* will eventually pull herself out of the gap. She'll set aside the mask of herself she's made to fit in the mirror of others' expectations and remember that true maturity comes from pursuing what we love best. In going always further up and further in.

In truth, it doesn't matter if you're a Susan or a Lucy, as long as, when you look in the mirror, you remember Ramandu's admonishment. What we are made of does not limit what we are. We're the ones who can do anything, save the world or break it.

The choice is ours.

⟶•⟩•⟩※⟨•⟨•⟵

Zu Vincent's novel *The Lucky Place* is published by Front Street Press and was an Honor Book for the 2009 Paterson Prize for Books for Young People. She holds an MFA in Writing from Vermont College of Fine Arts and is the author of the 2008 Scholastic biography *Catherine the Great: Empress of Russia*. Her work has also appeared in *The ALAN Review*, *Yoga Journal*, and *Harper's*, among others.

Kiara Koenig currently serves as adjunct English faculty and teaches creative writing and literature. She holds an MFA in Creative Writing as well as an MA in Literature from CSU, Chico. Her essays and poems have appeared in several journals and magazines, including *Watershed*, *The News & Review*, and *Peralta Press*.

Want *More* Smart Pop?

www.smartpopbooks.com

» Read a new free essay online everyday

» Plus sign up for email updates, check out our upcoming titles, and more